PENNINE TALES

PENNINE TALES

Henry Livings

Methuen

First published in 1983
by Methuen London Ltd
11 New Fetter Lane,
London EC4P 4EE
Copyright © Henry Livings 1983
Printed in Great Britain
by Richard Clay (the Chaucer Press) Ltd, Bungay, Suffolk
Filmset in Monophoto Imprint by
Northumberland Press Ltd, Gateshead

*The line drawings in the text
are by Maria Livings.*

British Library Cataloguing in Publication Data
Livings, Henry
    Pennine tales.
    I. Title
    823'.914[F]   PR6062.I/
    ISBN 0-413-53600-9

Acknowledgements

'Dog Race Coup', 'Transport Problem', 'Hanging Party', 'Local Funeral' and 'Bowls Handicap' were all first published in *The Guardian*.

'A Small Death' and 'A Stranger' were first broadcast on BBC Radio 4's 'Morning Story', and 'Twice-Nightly, Thursday Off to Learn It', 'Fit-Up Touring, Also to Help in Kitchen' and 'Will the Demon King Please Wear the Hat Provided?' on BBC Radio 4's 'Just After Four'.

Contents

DOG RACE COUP

Nobody outside this village ever believes me when I tell about Harpo, people think I've invented him. This is not so: Harpo invented himself. On the subject of wine, for instance, he knows there are three sorts: red, pink, and white. On this basis he will give you an extended account of wine and its uses, normally ending with 'I wouldn't give you tuppence for champagne; cider is every bit as adequate.' He's an expert on everything, and a rivetting anecdotalist; I won't spoil your meal, but his account of being taken short leaping a low wall in pursuit of the 183 bus, told with a semaphore of mime worthy of Marceau, and ending with the conductor remarking, 'My word, you'll have to get off this bus if anyone else wants to come on,' is a cherished classic.

Take the matter of his dog, Benji. 'It's definitely a Basenji,' he said, walking round the Co-op freezer with the animal sticking its nose into everything, 'ancient Egyptian hunting dog; I've seen a picture in a dog book, same curved tail; that's why we called it Benji, after the ancient Egyptian dog breed. Fastest dog in Ravensgill, even though it's had a broken leg.'

Why do we rise to such things? Why challenge obvious balderdash? Why not just let him rattle on? He's entertaining, original, a lunatic. How in the world would anyone get a Basenji out of the Dog's Home? Come to think of it, how come Harpo got his dog free when everyone else has to pay £7? Imponderables.

'Do me a favour,' I said, 'mine's a damn lurcher; that thing wouldn't have a chance. Get off.' (Benji was licking the butter packs and I was after buying some.)

'I'll definitely challenge any dog against mine,' he said.

'Get that stinking pooch out of here,' said Mr Bacon.

'D'you mind,' said Harpo, 'that's no pooch, it's a Basenji.'

The word got about. A small committee was formed, rules framed. No reference was made to broken legs, but it was to be for mongrels only (Harpo was wounded, but confident, after this slur), the length of the football pitch, and started with a shotgun blank by the landlord of the Tinker and Budget, entrance fee ten shillings. (We're waiting for the older end to die off before we introduce metrication.) The book was to be held by Nipper Schofield, well experienced in illegal book-making at bowls matches, known absconder. Once, when he was really in trouble, he phoned up the landlord of the other pub, the Shanter, from the kiosk outside, and stuck a pencil in his mouth, on a Sunday, mark.

'Peeppeeppeep ... Hallo? This is Mr Schofield's bank manager; he tells me he's cashed a cheque with you; he's asked me to tell you not to bother presenting it, he'll come in and settle it Monday.'

Another imponderable: what were we doing putting money into his hands? I suppose to a certain extent we relish the consistency of his depradations. Be it understood that no money was to change hands on the bets till after the race, but nevertheless. Everybody paid their entrance fee, except Harpo.

Blatantly furtive training sessions began; you could hardly go into the playing fields without someone speedily and casually pocketing a pigeon-watch or elaborately not looking at his digital as he threw a stick for a scampering ragmop. The women were the most obsessive: Mrs Hirst, fifteen stone and a compulsive nibbler who didn't like to leave the dog out, had a good half stone off her Labrador/Alsatian by switching from chocolate digestive biscuits to dogchews for its between-meals snacks, and throwing its ball down a banking for half an hour every day; she promised it verbally a biscuit if it won, but its eyes grew more desperate by the day and it had to go on Valium after the race.

Then there's Marrie, who's been going to obedience classes for four years. 'He's all right when there's other dogs, it's when you get him on his own he goes mutton-headed.' I saw her in a back lane; she'd devised a scheme whereby she was at one end of the course and her husband at the other, so that, when loosed, Duke had a quick decision to make as to which of its owners it was going to run away from.

In my opinion, my Bounty was the strongest entry, on the grounds of obedience: she comes to me when I call, and of course she was bred mostly for speed anyway. Early morning I sat her on the touchline, told her to stay, walked to the other end, called, and she ran to me. Nine seconds. Not world class, but good enough for the mutts of Ravensgill I thought, in my pride. The dog gave evidence that it thought I'd gone potty: where were the rabbits if it was required to run? On the fourth morning it lay down and yawned on the touchline, so I knocked off the training.

11.30 am. The football field. A prize of £9.50 (Harpo still hasn't paid). Starter and finishing judge in position. Nineteen dogs, from terrier-style to lolloping Labrador crosses (there's a large black dog on the estate that's *always* first on a bitch's doorstep). Every knuckle white. Maybe thirty spectators. Nipper in his dad's velour trilby, bawling the odds. No Harpo, no Benji.

He's chickened out. He'll be watching from behind the curtains at his Auntie Alice's. We shan't see him for weeks, until he thinks we've forgotten. It was like this when he was telling us about his skill at unarmed combat and then we found out that the husband of one of his paramours, a karate enthusiast from Ashton, was standing in the other bar.

11.45 Harpo comes, pale from Saturday, the dog on a brand new lead, steadily the length of the pitch, daughter Linda beside him, clearly wishing herself elsewhere, cheeks aflame. A crossword fanatic, he was delighted to find that 'crapulous' means poorly through the effects of drink. 'You'll have to excuse me, gentlemen,' he will say at a Sunday morning bowls match, 'I'm feeling a little crapulous today.'

'Benji's been sick,' he tells us by way of excuse, 'I told him he was in a race, and I had to wait while he was sick on the way down.'

He takes the lead off Benji, and Linda holds the animal among the competitors, by now strung like banjos. 'Come on, Benji,' he says, 'c'mon boy.'

Finishers set off for the other touchline.

'C'mon Benji, c'mon.'

'Shut it, Harpo, you drive us mad when you're not here, and you drive us mad when you're here.'

'It's my method, Henry. C'mon Benji!'

Finishers all in place, handlers in place, judge signals with white hankie, starter raises the shotgun. You can almost hear false teeth being tested to destruction. 'BOCK!' and they're off.

Twenty throats roar for their dogs, women screaming with unpent fury, urging the animals. Marrie's scheme falls to pieces at once: Duke runs away from the both of them, and is found at home later, staring with punished eyes from under the hen hut. Mrs Hirst's pudding dog leads the pack with joyous yelps, its mind mayhap on chocolate digestive biscuits. Benji well up and going strongly. Where the devil's Bounty? Good grief, she's run straight to the starter and sits, eager, ears up, bright and ready to be waved on to the rabbit. What did I have in my head to think I could call her in all this din? My wife dashes across to wave her on, frenzied, and the dog sets off, a blur of speed after the others. Can she make it through the pack?

They're bunching, and then bundling as the pudding dog wheels back, eager to be among its friends, Mrs Hirst's imprecations rising above the clamour like exploding rockets. Benji is through and over the line, passes Harpo at an easy gallop, across the road, and into the Tinker and Budget, it being opening time.

A SMALL DEATH

I have before me a skull, two and a quarter inches long; its brainpan narrows like a pear towards the brow, ribbed for strength in the shape of a T; the eye sockets are reversed capital Cs, the muzzle thick and sturdy, the long canine and eye-teeth clenched among neat tiny incisors and pre-molars, the molars rugged as mountains, the hinge of the jaw now unattached but broad and then tapering, a triangle to support a powerful strap of muscle. This was Gussie. A jill ferret, coffee cream with dark glossy tail and paws and a band of dark fur behind her head like a ruff, black bright button eyes. If you called, 'Gussiegussiegussiegussiegussie,' in imitation of her, and of all ferrets' chuckling noise, she would come questing out of her nest, or a rabbit burrow, her nose up, her back arched always like a tiny polar bear.

She was a hunting animal, but she was also my friend in her own way, with as much interest in scrambling up my clothes to nose about busily on my shoulder as in exploring the dark polished tunnels in search of rabbits to bolt into the receiving nets.

Many a ferret will peer suspicious and independent out of a burrow and retreat into darkness out of hand's reach as soon as you offer to pick them up. Gussie's idea, when she'd finished an enquiry, was to scurry out and clamber up me. She didn't stay there long; she didn't stay anywhere long that wasn't Houdini-proof, but she liked to say 'Hello ...' or maybe it was king-of-the-castle, and she didn't care who it was played hummock.

One thing for sure, if I had her in the house she would thud in perilous circles round my feet as I moved about, with occasional nosy sorties at the dogs or the cat. The cat is a malignant animal that bullies the dogs with indignant yowls, but even she made for high ground when Gussie came marching in. The dogs were trusting but cautious, and Gussie could have any old thing they happened to be chumbling at the time; they would lie or sit, rolling their eyes round to keep her in vision: a brief sniff at their bums and then on over the fat tail, leaving an impression of an exquisite canine tickle of embarrassment.

Saturday afternoon is dopey time at our house, and I took the coal hod upstairs into the sitting-room, opened the glass front of the stove and began riddling out the ashes, intending to light the fire and zed in front of it. Gussie had followed me upstairs and was hurtling round the skirting boards, exploring under furniture, climbing in a frenzy of energy over me as I crouched to my task, muttering and chuckling in little crescendos: her one meal of the day was due and where was it?

Looking back, I must have seen the grey-brown-ivory shadow pass me; at the time I was only consciously and briefly aware of a silence under my scraping at the ash and cinders. Paused, called out. No response, no scuttering. I went out onto the landing; down to the kitchen. Silence. If there was anyone there, they were incidental to my dizzy and mounting dismay. I didn't register their presence, only an absence, a blank silence. Back upstairs. Called again. Good grief she'd shot past me; it wasn't a curl of rising fine ash, it had been Gussie: the damn ferret had gone over the fire bars, through an impossible gap in the top firebrick, and she was in the chimney. It was the only place she could be.

I couldn't believe it and I had to believe it, clutching my head in disbelief, incomprehension. Pulled out the firebrick to uncover the hole leading to the stub of cast-iron flue. Shoved my hand gingerly in: she could just about turn in a three-inch diameter tube if I gave her the chance, and I didn't want to dislodge her into worse trouble. The chimney is five feet wide by two feet, made of any old brick, pebble or stone the Victorian brickie had to hand ... Hanging a picture at our house has its moments: one place the pin disappears into crumbling cement or even lime and horsehair plaster, and in another the pin returns like sling-shot at the man with the hammer. Downstairs it's bricked-up, with a gas-stove anchored in front of it. I listened. It's not possible. It's possible.

Some soot sprayed down in the dark. What disturbed it? The base of the chimney below must be stacked with sixteen years of soft dust and soot, unbreathable. But she's nimble. The inside of the chimney is rough ... any of the old cement rendering must have long flaked off.

I called. Again a spray of dust, but maybe my urgent voice disturbed it. The stove is plugged in with asbestos rope, not cemented, so I was able to draw it out on its flagstone base. 'Dumdumdumdumdum,' I called again, 'Gussiegussiegussiegussiegussie – c'monc'monc'mon.'

The light wind across the pots above stirred the dead air inside, nothing else. I thrust my hand in as far as it would go till I was soot and bloody scrapes up to my shoulder, trying to imagine what it looked like in there when we pulled out the old fireplace, moving my hand slowly and carefully for a touch of the fine curved set of claws, an inquisitive nose. I settled back, trying to think, and the dogs sniffed, each in its turn, unable to find anything but the stale sulphurous smell: one wag of the tail would have been something to go on, but no.

Leave the stove away from the chimney breast was the only chance; the children and my wife thought, and then didn't think, as I did, that they could hear her shifting minutely. And all the time the leaden thought of that soft, deep pile of dead, suffocating ash below. Listened below at the wall behind the gas stove. Listened, and called, at a still-open, twin chimney-stack in the next room: she could have clambered up the slope to where the other one joins. Maybe a noise, maybe the faint rattle of dust falling, maybe not. Certainly the wind high above, emphasizing the silence.

Four hours later, in a benumbed gloom, we accepted that quite ordinary things still had to be done: the dogs walked, supper cooked and eaten, and, worst of all, the stove replaced, and lit.

Ferrets, like the rabbits they hunt, move at approximately four hour intervals. She never lay up, but if some other ferret ever kills-down, I block the hole and come back four hours later, rather than waste my breath trying to call off a hunter busy gorging itself and deaf to the world above.

The movements in the chimney we'd hoped were Gussie were no longer detectable.

If you've ever lost an animal that was part of your daily life, you'll know the extraordinary void such a disappearance leaves, the ghostly face that appears bright and quick to the imagination, at a window, opening the door on a darkened room, behind the mesh of an empty hutch. The feeding-bowl, useless.

Gussie was dead.

I work at home, in the sitting-room, and it's wintertime I'm talking about; the stone walls of the hillsides marked by traces of frozen snow, the valley dank and misty. The following week, Wednesday, I checked the sitting-room stove as usual in the morning. If it was still in from the previous evening I would fill the hod and keep it going, low, for my day's work: otherwise put on a thick jersey and re-light it later when I had the leisure.

The hod was empty; I picked it up, flicked open the glass door; the warmth of the firebricks rose in the room, but inside just dead ash with maybe one dull ember. I let it fall closed and turned to leave the room. A puff of ash plumed up behind the fire-darkened glass. Perhaps hunting has given me wrap-around vision to compensate for my blurred eyesight, but, I swear it, I caught it. I went back to the stove for another quick look.

I'd dropped the hod and gathered Gussie into the crook of my arm before I'd properly understood what was happening: she was *there*, on the ashes, she was *alive*. Saturday, Sunday, Monday, Tuesday, night and day, without food or water, she'd perched somewhere in that terrible fume-filled chimney, and there she was; thin, weak, but eye-bright; nose hard and dry, one back paw burned so that she couldn't move it, the hair matted together and crisp where it had been silky. For a moment my mind spun round.

Water, yes, just a little from the kettle; she took it from my palm, the long pink tongue, rough, easing out, moving her body as little as possible, curled on my arm still. Break a cod liver oil capsule, I don't care if I stink all day, also on my hand. I fed and watered dogs and cat, a major policing job with each longing to gobble up the other's food, made myself a pot of tea and drank it, without Gussie being moved from that curled nest in clean air.

There being no white to her eyes, no apparent iris, it was hard to tell whether she looked about, but it seemed not . . . more as if she concentrated all her wasted energy inwards, still and patient. There seemed no grit in her nose or mouth, and, impossible as it was, she'd retained enough in her tear ducts for the eyes to be protected. I finally put her back in the hutch, taking out the wooden partition that divided nest from run, so that she could get to her water bottle and the raw egg I broke into her bowl.

The end of this story is vile. If you like happy endings, leave it at this point. If, like me, you are astonished and impressed every time anew at life, and death, and find the survival of even so simple a creature awe-inspiring and sufficient, then stay with my happy ending to the anecdote: the rest, even I would prefer not to know.

My wife first met death personally when a young sparrow we tried to rescue after a cat had mauled it died on her hand; she was overwhelmed by the fine and finite distinction between a heart fluttering and a heart still, the instantaneous clouding and closing of a bright eye. So it is, we share mortality with the rest of animal creation, and it's as grand as Doomsday every time.

Gussie was completely recovered inside six weeks; she hunted well, and was as frantic for attention every time you passed the hutch as she was before; scaled the heights of Mount Me and peeked about, claws in my hair; hurled herself as recklessly down my slopes as ever; persecuted the cat with the same cold enthusiasm; inspected the dogs as they sat quivering; risked my lumbering feet with her wild circular ritual food dance.

I got a mate for her – jill ferrets get ill or don't live to any age unless they breed – and in June she produced three live kits. One dead. I didn't know it, of course, but the dead kit was the first tolling of a long knell. Something had stayed with her from the chimney, some darkness: now, she would sink her teeth into any human hand except mine. If you want to teach them not to bite, don't draw your hand away, no matter how great the temptation is when they're into you deep as the gums. Push back to the molars firmly; you'll be no worse wounded and they learn rapidly that they're wasting their time. This training instruction, I should warn you, doesn't apply when it's your ear they've got gripped. But with Gussie, and except for me, no hand or ankle escaped, and not just a nip either; whereas before her ordeal she would tolerate the roughest handling.

Then I found the second kit dead. Not thrown out as a runt: murdered. Possibly Gussie's milk had gone back, though she seemed full enough; certainly the remaining two didn't thrive. Then another kit was killed. It wasn't the hob ferret: I took the survivor and put it with him in another hutch, hand-rearing the kit; and father proved attentive and careful. Even though the kit had to be fed far more frequently than him, he showed nothing but busy concern, insisting that it sleep with him curled round it, dashing anxiously about as I fed it, licking it tidy when I returned it.

And still Gussie savaged everyone who went near enough. It was useless my trying to get her to nip me and then teaching her different, she wouldn't: she wanted to tear the world to pieces, not me. I couldn't leave her with anyone, to feed her, or clean out her hutch. If I was away for more than twenty-four hours my son or my wife had scarlet wounds to show me. If we all went away, no chance of asking a neighbour to look after her.

And so, the only hand she trusted, the hand that had lifted her up after her terrible punishment, that same hand took her gently out and up the garden, stroked her for the last time, and as swiftly as I know how, broke her neck.

TRANSPORT PROBLEM

Dog's Doogle Eye in his young brother's Pluto mask is not greatly altered in appearance, though admittedly slightly more menacing. Well, eerie. He walked up to the teller's window, pointed the Mauser water-pistol at the security glass with a steady hand.

'Give me the money,' he said, 'I want the money, all of it.'

Since he was wearing the jersey she'd knitted him for Christmas, his Auntie Doris had no trouble identifying the robber. 'Don't be so silly, Stuart,' she said, pressing the alarm button just in case. 'You never know these days,' she said later, 'with the people there is about.' She carefully and deliberately emptied the cash drawer, humouring a madman; a fair assessment.

The police siren is no great sensation in Ravensgill: since we went into Manchester Harry Mooney's feeling for the grandeur of the peace officer's role has reached new decibel levels, and anyway it helps him get home for his tea down the narrow lanes without hold ups, except for tractors. Nobody even looked out of their window as Dog scrambled out of the bank, scattering pound notes and loose change as he straddled the getaway bike and pedalled in a lather of determination towards the canal bridge, the low setting of the saddle and the fury of his action giving an impression of more legs and arms than would be appropriate to the one person.

There was a moment or two before Harry and his colleague came round to rightly believing this vision, time for Dog to reach the bridge, abandon a futile attempt to negotiate his machine through the stile-hole, and then throw himself down the steps to the towpath; and then when they'd recovered there was the problem of the trail of cash.

'Don't worry about the money,' called Doris, 'I'll pick it up; I've nobody in just now. It's our Stuart.'

'Is it?' said Harry.

'He's always been a bit addled,' she said.

'I was just having a brew,' said Harry.

'There's always something, isn't there,' said Doris, gasping as she stooped to retrieve the money.

They caught up with Dog's Doogle Eye after a brief, mud-spattered chase. It took more time to fish the notes out of the canal, a tedious business in which Dog was no help. He got three years. You'll think I'm speaking of a habitual criminal perhaps, but the only other time I can recall him actually thieving was when he was wheeling his brother's pram down Pin Lane, an unusual sight, which PC Mooney, on foot in those days, remarked.

'Whatever are you doing, Stuart?' he said.

'Just taking the baby for a walk,' said Doogle Eye, letting go the handle briefly and setting the brake.

The pram strained at the brake, tilted, broke loose, and careered off down the hill with gathering momentum, veered as it reached maximum speed, hit the kerb and dis-integrated, spilling a hundredweight or more of lead from various roofs which Harry was about to investigate.

His father insisted on speaking up for him in court. In spite of Dog's objections, the magistrate thought he could accept a character witness. 'Send him down your honour,' offered Dad, 'he's been a scab on my back for twenty-five years, send him down!' He got a suspended sentence.

Transport has always been a problem for Dog, and for

24

his mate, Harpo. Between them, they must have had and caused more trouble to and with motor bikes than twenty years of TT races. Harpo never seemed to be out of plaster, or at least a bandage. They would buy a bike between them, the investment being too much for either of them on their own. An interesting spectacle as they cruised sedately together, Dog shouting hysterical driving instructions, selling Rugby Club draw tickets in the back streets of Oldham.

It fascinated me that, although they normally both got on, it was always Harpo that broke a leg. And he doesn't seem all that bad a driver; Dog's Doogle Eye, on the other hand, drives like he thinks, in a whirlwind of error. Mind, barring the evidence of Harpo's knees, knuckles and elbows, and the appalling noise when Dog's in the driving seat, there's never been any objective test of their competence: neither has a licence.

Harry has considered arresting Harpo, but whenever he gets round to considering it, Harpo is between bikes. Dog doesn't come into it, he doesn't live in Ravensgill. And anyway, there's the problem of the prison population. 'Strangeways is no place for Harpo,' Harry will say, 'there's some very unpleasant people in there; if I could get him into Broadmoor it'd make more sense and justice.'

Harry is a real policeman. The vagaries of police policy, from Panda car to foot patrol, from Special Action Group to community care, could be graphed, and might well be represented as a silhouette of Afghanistan, but Harry's instinctual and compassionate approach would be a steady, level, unalterable horizon.

Harry's custom of drinking in the Shanter caused the Inspector some anguish; he had to concede that Harry's compendious knowledge of village affairs was useful, he just wished he wouldn't seek the information on duty.

He decided it had to stop: he mounted guard personally, in mufti, over the constable's bike, parked as it was outside the Shanter, for one hour twenty-five minutes by the Co-op clock. At 3.25 pm a small boy took charge of the police bicycle.

'Where d'you think you're going with that, sonny? That's police property.'

'I know,' said the child, 'Mr Mooney's given me fivepence to take it home for him.'

Harry had been in the Tinker and Budget.

It says something for Harpo's phenomenal energy that he mends well; after the third fracture in the one year, his wife, Maggie, decided that this particular saga had gone on long enough, besides which she was good and fed up of the current bike's presence in the hallway, rusting, dripping oil, and brooding darkly on the next damage it would inflict on her husband. A ragbone man came by and she quickly concluded a deal, even helping the man to hoist the machine on to his wagon. She set about scrubbing the lino clean of accumulated and congealed sump oil.

Harpo came home from the Bowls Club, arm in sling. 'Where's the bike got to?'

'I sold it.'

'What a good do; Dog's Doogle Eye will be highly delighted; he's nò good without me on the rugby tickets, and he's quite short just now. I'll give him one third, I think. How much did you get?'

'Thirty bob,' she said.

'WHAT?'

Harpo stepped forward, on to the bar of soap, spun down the hall with an ascending yell of alarm, bounced off the cellar door and broke his other collar bone.

The difference between Harpo and Dog is largely that Harpo never tells lies. I wouldn't be able to report these events if he didn't tell the world of his humiliations. He will confide the most wounding intimacies: his farts, for instance, are full of openly admitted risk.

'I'm afraid I'm going to have to go and have a look; excuse me.'

On the other hand, Dog's life-style is an elaborate, tautly-drawn fabric of lived mendacity. He acquired a brand-new motorbike, and managed to maintain that he'd paid cash for it, while at the same time evading Harpo's requests for his share of the rugby ticket money on the grounds that (a) they were being difficult at the Club; (b) he'd had a lot of back-rent to pay; and (c) his Giro cheque hadn't come.

'Your lips are moving again,' said Harpo.

A weird figure appeared at our front door one Tuesday evening, crash helmet like a Teuton warrior. I should have known him by the wrinkles in his hand-washable safari suit, but I reached for a walking stick. 'It's me, Stuart,' it said.

'Oh,' I said.

He took off the helmet. 'Is Harpo here? I've got a new bike.'

'No,' I said.

'Only he's generally here Tuesdays. I've got this new bike.'

Harpo comes round Tuesdays often enough; we play chess; if he wins, I get out the home-brewed wine. Then he loses.

'I won't come in,' said Dog, 'I thought Harpo'd be interested in my new bike.'

I shut the door on him, he can get me to screaming pitch fast.

Harpo was in the front room. 'I came in through the back, I hope you don't mind. Are we having a game of chess?'

'Dog's been here just, looking for you. He's got a new bike.'

'I know. Nictitating twat.'

'Nictitating' is Harpo's word of the month; apparently it means eye-twitching; with Dog everything twitches, so it's about right. I went to the shelf for the board and pieces.

Outside in the road, Dog's Doogle sat on the bike, facing the house, revving the motor, proud, preoccupied. I stopped in my track to watch through the window; Harpo sensed my sudden attention and came to my side. Such vibrant idiocy is hypnotic. Dog seemed to see us through the mist of scratches on his visor, he straightened, revved again. It sounded like a Harrier jet.

'Heaven's to Betsy, it's a branny,' said Harpo. Awestruck, he raised a hand in greeting and salute to his friend. His friend raised his hand in acknowledgement, a Roman emperor. The gesture released the clutch which he'd been holding out, and the bike took off for the house with a fierce snarl, one to forty in 1.25 seconds, and a wheelie to boot. Harpo and I ducked to one side, he seemed to be coming straight for the window. The house shook with the impact, it could have been a Leyland bus. As we rose, cautious, Dog was departing, slower, but still mobile, the buckled spokes and forks taking him in a series of corkscrew swoops, legs splayed.

Harpo began setting up the chessboard.

'You need transport,' he said, 'but I've had enough of motor bi-cycles, they can be extremely dangerous objects. I'm going to save up for an auto-mobile. Not a banger, a decent one, 'bout forty pounds.'

HANGING PARTY

Bet, secretary to Ravensgill dyeworks, has a voice like the sound of a tin can rolling back and forth in a flagged yard. Pressing creditors who phone the works start back from the receiver with wounded eardrums. Harpo came into the office to ask her for a toilet roll. She told him they'd had one last week and what happened to that?

Harpo winced. 'Madam,' he said, 'there are some twenty hairy recta out there, and they all need servicing.'

At fifty-one, she has a full, rounded, soft figure, glossy dark red hair cut short, lustrous brown almond eyes. Her husband died early, a happy man in all respects; in her presence, old men vibrate, and young men grow sombre. She got the toilet roll from among light bulbs in the safe. 'I don't know why you can't all go at home,' she said.

When you're working on the perch (two men draw the cloth out flat, looking for faults in the dyeing, then fold it for the baler), there isn't much to think about, you fall into reverie; especially if you've got Bulk opposite you, a putty-complexioned twenty-five stone (a guess, this, weighing machines mostly only go up to twenty-five stone, and he refuses to get on the weighbridge), whose idea of a witty rejoinder is a sullen 'You must be joking.'

He was demolishing a house for Jack Ledbury, and Jack came to see how the work went. 'Where's the gas meter?'

'You must be joking.'

'That's a criminal offence, that is, it's property of the Gas Board. I'll get the police, they'll soon find it, and it'll have your fingerprints on it.'

'They won't find my fingerprints on it, I punced it off the wall with my boot.'

Howf, dreaming on the perch, kept his gaze away from Bulk's, hoping for happier things to come into his mind. Harpo passed, bearing the toilet roll like a hard-won trophy.

Howf called out: 'What's she wearing today?'

'The dark green embroidered linen blouse, patent leather belt with gilded filigree buckle, black velvet skirt with lace-trimmed petticoat, black patent sling-back high heels.'

Howf groaned gently and rocked a little. 'Howf' is a word Howf invented. Not even he knows exactly what it means. He uses it, with an expressive lexicon of gesture, to indicate enthusiasm, somebody else's anger, the speed of some sudden event, a variety of emphasis. I passed the dyeworks wall on my midday walk. He stood there, a clean-shaven, fair-haired El Greco, his saint-like eyes fixed on the blue morning while raised voices came from within the open dock doors.

'All right, Howfie?'

He raised his hands like two ducks to face each other, opening and shutting fingers against thumbs in snap-pish colloquoy, and jerked his head towards the dye-works building, from which the angry clash of buckets could now be heard. 'Howf,' he said.

One other thing, he's hung like a bunch of Cumber-land sausages.

I'm told that the size of a man's parts has no relevance to masculine value; well, all right, but midnight in the graveyard can be unsettling as you search for the cat, reluctant to be woken at four am by piteous yowls; you listen intently in the silent inky dark, and then suddenly an eldritch wail of joy floats up from behind John Henry Buckley's headstone.

'G'night Howfie,' I said, when my heart had stopped knocking to get out.

'G'night Henry,' he said, 'how did you know it was me?'

He's also good to be *with*. The Ledburys graze several raggedy bits of land about the village, and Howfie and I were among others helping to pick up and house the hay one glittering July day. Twelve-year-old David Ledbury was waving a wrench at his bellowing grandad, and telling him what a effing old whatsit he was and how he couldn't drive a effing tractor and to effing get off and effing let someone on who effing could. Howf smiled peacefully out from a halo of hay and seeds: 'I like working for Jack,' he said, 'you always get a few breaks.'

However I still think it's female curiosity, at the least, that brings Howfie such quantities of sensual fulfilment.

He split the inside seam of his trousers somehow. Bulk offered to sew it up with a baling needle, an instrument which is about ten inches long, with a curved, blade-shaped point. Howfie considered briefly and declined; Bulk has a malign streak which Howf couldn't altogether trust in this sensitive area. 'I'll see what Bet can do for me.'

Bulk fell to brooding; even his sluggish imagination stirs at the thought of Bet. When he came to, Howf had gone, his spindly figure soon lost in the dense steam. 'You must be joking,' murmured Bulk, his lips moist.

The vessels whirred and clanked, trollies trundled, Bulk brooded on, motionless. Mr Mann came out of the steam: 'Have you gone dormant? You look like an advanced case of sleeping sickness.'

'I'm supposed to be perching, but Howf's split his trousers.'

Mr Mann tried recklessly to make sense of it, and gave up, more or less simultaneously, he had his heart to think about: 'I need someone to start number three.'

'I haven't got my prodder, I'm perching.'

'What for d'you need a prodder?'

Bulk didn't know; everybody always used a wooden stick to press the starter button of number three, that's all he knew.

'Come here,' said Mr Mann, rubbing at the rising pains in his chest, 'this is a dyeing vessel, it's at simmer, the roller above will rotate the cloth when you press the starter button. If you don't, I shall very soon have a piece of cloth which is half yellow and half white. Then you can watch so's it doesn't tangle: it'll be fun for you.'

Bulk looked at him doubtfully. Mr Mann peered at the button, which was indeed difficult of access, sunk back and corroded in its socket. He snatched a pencil from his overall coat with a trembling hand and jabbed it into the socket. The rollers clattered into action, the power shot up the graphite of the pencil and Mr Mann crossed the alley backwards at hallucinatory speed, to thud into a stanchion, sliding to its base, a shower of rust powdering his ashen face. Mr Mann sat in a heap, still. Bulk thought he'd better see what Bet could do, but Mr Mann had a point, it was fun all right.

Bet screeched quietly at Howfie that she hadn't got such a thing as a needle and thread, but she'd see what she could do with paperclips. She knelt to her task, the office silent. Occasionally, as she punctured and clipped the trouser leg, she jangled out some pleasantry, like, 'The one thing nobody thieves from this place is paper-clips: no wonder we have to lock up light bulbs.' But Howfie was struggling with the image of her round, entrancing shoulders, the wisp of down at her neck; he concentrated on the time-clock, which he could just make out through the window on to the corridor. It's a sturdy old machine, which has survived being pushed back to ten to eight, and on to six o'clock (for the overtime), every day, and can still manage a desultory click or two in its efforts to connect with real, as against fantasy time.

As she passed his knee on the way up, the paperclips increasing in frequency until they were two per inch, he moved his mind urgently to the time he caught himself in his zip in the gents at Failsworth; he relived the terrible decision, whether to go on or to go back; a faint whimper escaped his lips. Bet looked up at his martyred face, her eyes wide, a faint dew on her delicate upper lip, her bosom swept with compassion.

By the time he got Mr Mann to the office, Bulk was in a worse state than his boss, who was still shaken, but able to talk: 'Where's Bet?'

Bulk gasped speechless in the only chair.

'I think I'll be all right now; I'll just sit down for a bit. Go and see to number three.'

'You must be joking.'

'The place is deserted, is it opening time? Can't be opening time, nobody came to me for a sub.' Mr Mann was getting feverish, the loneliness was unnerving: one can be an island, Bulk is the tundra. 'Where's Howf? Don't answer, I've already had an answer, and I didn't understand it.'

Bulk stirred; Mr Mann massaged his chest, his eyes staring; Bulk worked it out, slowly, that he'd be better off standing gazing at number three, and lumbered off.

Mr Mann passed him on his way to the warehouse, morosely contemplating the bedraggled piece, tangled beyond rescue. 'It wants an hour at simmer; is Howf back on the perch?'

'You must be joking.'

'Where's Harpo?'

'He's on the bog.'

'It'll have to stop, all these toilet rolls.'

In the warehouse, Bet, spreadeagled among bales under Howfie, confused about certain things but not about this. Her dimpled knees would have brought tears of happiness to the eyes of angels, but the pure beauty of the scene was wasted on Mr Mann, he needed a focus for his pain: 'Howfie! You're finished!'

Howf raised eyes unblemished by the concept of sin. 'You're telling a lie there Mr Mann, I haven't.'

WOMAN ASSAULTS
DAUGHTER

Thirty-five years on, and in her mid-sixties, May Cadwell has an angular grace, with a fine-boned Roman profile. In her youth and in love she blazed with a swift glory that shook your heart like an earth tremor. Her eyes are a very light grey, her hair now thin and drawn back close to her head. She has a way of turning her face away and down in private consideration of good news – maybe the Christmas pension bonus, or there's a coach-trip organized to look at a famous garden – and I, for one, scour my memory for more good news, for a repeat of such a complete and uncomplicated movement.

The fresh gurgle of her laughter as she and I, partners at a whist drive, put down a sequence of doomed cards, to end up losing thirteen nil, had the pair of us in tears of hysteric happiness; our opponents glum with incomprehension. The best whist drive I ever was at, and only because of that one daft game at the one table. Mind, I've a notion it was the same evening I trumped my partner's ace of clubs; the Whistling Cowboy, whose unending breathy tuneless fluting ruckles my sanity, plays like an automatic card-dispensing machine; and I think I renegued, too, to trump in. Our opponents took it calmly enough, and Cowboy has no intellectual mechanism to interrupt his reflex flow of play and take note that I had not in fact run out of clubs. He stopped whistling, his lips pursed like a sow's arse, stared at his demolished ace, gathered it up, and went on playing with redoubled lack of concentration. He didn't speak to me for a fortnight either, so you could say it was a treble treat: his breath smells of putrid meat.

May invariably wears a chiffon scarf, lilac or pale green, pinned at the neck with a silver horseshoe brooch, like a gypsy or a horse-coper. I also know she has a fine pearly white line right across her throat. So does everybody else that knows her at all. She walks with her arms turned out, a free gait, striding, quite fast for a country woman. You get the impression that if there were to be some good experience, May would be walking towards it, arms wide, reckless of opinion. She'd've beaten the snake to the apple.

Her mother was one of the village's two butchers, the best I ever came across in three continents. She did all her own slaughtering, until the law was altered, and all her own buying. Widowed in 1919, she ran the tiny slaughterhouse and the shop, and brought up her daughter, as she had done during her husband's army service; a mottled, stubby figure in flowered pinafore, mobcap and clogs, dragging a bullock down by a rope through a ring in the floor to its nose, tying off, driving the poleaxe in clean and true, and puddling the dead animal's brains with a cane. She could kill and dress out a pig as fast as two men, and was in demand for illicit slaughter during rationing. She would either kill or dress out: two visits by a butcher to the same farmhouse had the police dropping in, casual.

She went to Cowboy's house late one Saturday, by request. 'Where's the pig?'

'It's in the barn.'

They went across. The pig scuttered off a heap of corn bags to greet them. 'I thought you said you'd kill it.'

'I will,' said Cowboy, and produced a gigantic service revolver, taking aim at the joyous scampering pig. Mrs

Cadwell clomped for the door. 'Don't worry, love, I wain't hit thee!'

'That's a true word, thou bleeding wain't: I s'all not be here!'

That's how Cowboy got his name, among other things.

Meat ration coupons were never very seriously negotiable in the village, what with nocturnal pigs, poultry, rabbits, hares, and a long list of 'casualty killings' – farmers were and are allowed to slaughter damaged beasts to put an end to their pain. When Alan stayed at the big house and came into Cadwell's for a couple of sausages in exchange for some wellworn scraps of ration book, there was a baffled conversation between May and him that only ended when Mrs Cadwell bustled out of the cold room and told him piss off with his ration book and his sausages too. He had a fine, neatly trimmed Vandyke beard, unusual for 1946, deep-set amber-coloured eyes, well-cut tweeds and a brown trilby, polished brown brogues. Maybe forty-five.

Can you be 'in love' with someone you've known every single day of your life? I think not; it requires the excitement of discovery, the tilting of humdrum experience to the bright brief flare of novelty. Girls in our village can be stately queens, handsome; we watch the pill fill them out and make them over into womanhood, a secret initiation. It's a modern tragedy that our menfolk have no such ceremony of manhood, except the pub or the Club, or maybe bowls or cricket. Those who fall in love incline to find outsiders. My observation is not scientific, but disasters with outsiders are not significantly more common than with locals.

Howfie Whitehead's sexual enthusiasms, as he grows older, begin to look like a lifetime's commitment to the entire female population ... 'Lervely,' he says, his eyes searching the top of his skull, his long hands describing

Rubensesque improbabilities; but he's never been in love.

May was on Raven's Nab in the falling light when they met; Alan on an idle evening's walk, she on a breathless, giddy errand of hope. The rocks of the Nab rise, slab by slab of blackened and wind-scoured sandstone, out of the peat and heather. In the late spring a vixen screams there for the fox like an endlessly strangled woman; the wind is steady, but there's shelter among polished sheepwalks. Alan stopped and stared, wooden: her rosy fluster in the shop had certainly seemed to have been his fault. 'Are these all right for a few sausages?'

'You can have a few sausages.'

'Good, I'll have a few.'

'Pound? Two pound?'

'What's two pound? Two – four sausages?'

'Two is two.'

'You: piss off with your sausages, and your blether.'

What compass is it in the human head that directs us to those we need/wish/have to meet? She had no conscious reason to suppose that that was where he would be. She knows the village stone by stone; he was a stranger. Where would a stranger go to stroll and fill in a couple of empty hours? It was as if time froze inside her mind, and the chance that their paths would cross was an ice-crystal with myriad facets, dazzling, intricate, accurate: without the need for calculating, she walked in the one direction, his.

Howfie heard them over the wall and walked on, shivering, as he returned without his underpants from an assignation with his thick-legged 'un in Jack Ledbury's haybarn; Cowboy saw them as he lifted his rabbit snares; May, standing mother-naked in the heather, arms spread, moonlight silver glittering across her strong shoulders, sparkling in her hair, her voice a whisper in the air.

'Now will you remember me?'

Cowboy never spoke of it as long as he lived, he had no words for such a sight; and Mrs Cadwell saw it with eyes suffused with blood, her broad fist pressed flat on the iron mantelshelf, watching the kitchen range burn even, hour by barren hour. It was as if the village committed itself to May's consummation, much loved, much loved.

Alan stood in the darkened yard behind the shop; May said to wait, and she'd bring him in for a cup of tea and a biscuit; mother would still be up. It's inconceivable she didn't see the effect she had on her mother's burdened and battened mind; her hair every whichway, her eyes bright, dotty and bewitched, her cheeks glowing and smudged, her blouse streaked with the purple of the peat. It's conceivable.

In the mother, twenty-seven years of hard, lonely labour, the scrubbing, the gloss-painting, the late-night counting-up, half-day closing spent watching her husband, week after week, cough away the rags of his mustard-gassed lungs over basket-work in Broughton Hospital. A stretcher-bearer, nobody knew what the gas could do, did do. The few days of their marriage, that brought her one trace of unsullied happiness: May, joyfully born on the day of the breaking of the Hindenberg Line, a fulfilment. Now she had £12,000 saved, a respected business, and her mouth was full of ash. A stranger's soft hand lay on her money, on May, who could no more dress out a carcase than fly in the air.

The knives lay on the block, scoured and sharpened for the following day; May's job, which her mother had done, in sullen resentful obstinacy.

'I've been walking out mother.'

'I know. Thou'rt a slut. Thou meetst him just and thou'rt out in a field with him.'

'I want him to come in and meet thee properly. I've said I'll brew up for him. He's a nice man.'

The ancient unstained blade missed the jugular vein by a millimetre each side. May didn't move. Her breath whistled through the half-severed windpipe, blood pearled bright as a pigeon's across her round white throat and the soiled blouse. Had it been a lamb or a pig the woman would have had it on a steel hook with one swift lift; instead she thrust open the door on the yard, and bayed her pain into the dark, the heavy knife rattling on the stone flags: 'There thou, art thou bloody man, see now what thou'st made me do.'

EVER UPWARDS

Ravensgill is a terminus. Harpo was getting off the single-decker, I was getting on. The city drivers are maddened by the schedules, which are the same as when they had conductors to take the fares; they hate the villages, our 'Good mornings', 'How's the leg?' and such, every fare stage a social ceremony.

'What an experience,' said Harpo.

'Are you getting on or getting off ?' said the driver. 'I want this door shut.' He shut it.

'Eighty pence,' I said, 'all the way, please. What experience?'

'I want to get off,' said Harpo. The driver operated the door. 'I knew if I waited long enough you'd make up your mind.'

The bus wasn't due out, and I wanted to hear about the experience, so I followed him off. The driver shut the door.

'Look at the state of me.' Now I could see him fully: every pocket bulged like a herring net. 'I said to the driver when I got on, Good Heavens, I said, I shall have to abandon thoughts of travelling on this omnibus, I only seem to have a ten pound note upon my person. Do not concern yourself, good sir, he says, I can most certainly accommodate you.' Harpo held on to his lapels to support the weight of cupro-nickel and copper the driver had off-loaded on to him.

The driver sat hunched over his clipboard, isolated in

bitterness, four miles from the nearest cup of tea.

'I'm catching this bus,' I said.

'Did I ever tell you about Dog's Doogle Eye and the fifty pence piece on the bus?' he said.

'No,' I said, 'and you're not going to now.' I picked up some stray penny pieces and handed them to him, they seemed to be dripping from him.

'The dog must have torn the pocket as well; what a vicious animule.'

'Which dog's that?'

'Pardon?' he said; he'd spotted another penny.

The side-slips in Harpo's narratives always catch me off-guard; they may be intended to nail attention more firmly, or perhaps he wants to fill out his mythology, like a Renaissance ceiling; I tried to hold the dog in my head, but the pale quivering image of Doogle took over. Harpo shares his every job with him, perhaps for the myth.

Once, Doogle called on Harpo: 'Good evening, sir or madam,' he said, 'I wonder if I could interest you in a major financial proposition which will establish your security and that of your family for life?'

'Erm, it's me, Harpo,' said Harpo, 'we're acquainted.'

'Is there some handy hostelry where we could discuss my proposition? Sir.'

Harpo glanced back into the house and round about in the street, in case Doogle was addressing a third party he hadn't so far noticed: 'D'you want a cup of tea? And d'you mind not calling me sir? I keep thinking it's the bum bailiff again.'

'If I could just jot down a few entirely confidential details,' Doogle went on, mouthing the patter over to himself before uttering it, like a film slightly out of sync, 'with the aid of the information you supply I can formulate a plan appropriate to your particular finances.' After this manner, the poor and feckless are set to prey on the poor and feckless. 'Ah, come on, Harpo, do us a favour, you're my first call; I'll buy you a pint of bitter.'

'Only if you stop calling me sir.'

Doogle's urgent whisper blew about in the doorway like dry leaves: 'I got to, it's how you have to do it. Don't let me down.'

Harpo bought the beer; Doogle spread out his papers, took out his biro. 'What is your full name and marital status, sir?'

'God damn it, Doogle, we've known each other for twenty year!'

Doogle wrote steadily, the spidery blue lines spreading over the page like a railway network. It's not that he's semi-literate, or stupid; on the contrary, he's quite intelligent; it's mostly that he doesn't know what's going on, except that somewhere, somehow, money is going to pass by, some of which he will grab: it's a natural law. The inside of his head must be like a swarm of midges over an underground water course: busy, knowing there must be a reason for all this activity, but unable, through all the busyness, to find out what it is.

'What is your trade or profession sir?'

'Out of work. You wittering prawn.'

'Previous employment or office?'

'Plastics extrusion engineer.' Harpo sat up, wondering with furtive glee how Doogle would negotiate 'extrusion' when he got to it.

Doogle chewed at the biro in an ecstasy of mental block. 'How d'you spell plastics?' he said.

The driver opened the door: 'D'you want on this bus, pal?'

'What were you saying about the dog?' I said.

'You know me and Doogle are on the first-aid boxes? Well, I have this system: if nobody answers the front door, it's always a good idea to beetle round nice and steady to the back.' He demonstrated the strutting pace of a clockwork doll, elbows working, the change in his pockets thumping against his shanks, round the corner of the bus shelter and back. The driver's mouth slowly opened and closed on a wordless comment. 'Often enough, housewives will be gathered at the hedge, keenly watching and having a little discussion as to what you might be up to, and making up their minds between themselves they aren't going to open the door to you. Once my keen eye finds them, my spellbinding spiel can work its magic on their minds. Slight drizzle.'

I flicked an involuntary glance to the sky.

He was already giving the three steps up to a front door. Knock knock on the bus shelter window: 'Always make it sound like an expected friend. Anybody bringing a warrant of distraint or coming to cut off the gas is liable to be nervous and give it the ratatatat.' He peered into the next window: 'No sign of life, telly inert, used cup and saucer on glass-topped table. From last night.'

'This is you and Doogle on the knocker?'

'Yes: the most silent, the most deserted estate ever known to man, the Marie Celeste in Accrington brick. Move round path to back for survey of gardens.'

The bus driver had to crane round in his seat to watch Harpo come down the three steps and trot round an imaginary path, arms akimbo, his back arched with bright confidence.

'A small, most perfectly savage dog absolutely launched itself at me, chest level. I spun round in my terror, and leapt down the rockery, rock to rock, with the sound of rending fabric in my ears. I sat, absolutely trembling in the van, till Doogle came back.' His fingers described the flight, Incy Wincy Spider moonwalking; the driver picked his nose, mesmerized.

'It was the most dismal estate. Doogle got nothing,

mind he never does much: he says his teeth make him gag; would you rush to purchase first-aid boxes from a chap who clatters his teeth out of a polythene bag prior to addressing you? He's totally useless.'

'I know that full well, I just wonder why you ever have him with you. I can remember the time when he said he'd lost the calls record, stolen out of a telephone box God save the mark, and claimed half your calls at the office on the grounds he couldn't remember who'd sold which. Why d'you bother at all?'

'You've got to have a companion, haven't you? Anyway, I managed a few sales, enough for liquid refreshment and a pork pie. I says, tonight I shall go back to that house with the dog, and I *shall* make a sale, guaranteed; I shall tell them their dog tore my trousers, and they can hardly refuse a first-aid box. Oh yes, I was going to tell you about the fifty pence piece on the bus.'

'I'm not going to listen; what about going back to the house with the dog?'

'He saw this fifty pence piece on the top floor of the bus, and not wanting to be seen picking it up, he put his foot on it until such time as he could appropriate it discreetly. People were having to step over, or ease round this knee sticking out into the aisle; he could see conversations going on as to whether he was unfortunately formed or whether it was an artifical limb. By the time he got to his stop he had hot stabbing pains in his groin, cramp in the calf muscles, and no sensation whatsoever in his foot. He limped down the steps like Long John Silver and off the bus, and stood on the pavement waiting for the circulation to be restored so that he could proceed homewards without falling over. Then he realized he hadn't picked up the fifty pence piece.'

Arthur Lees, greengrocer, arrived in the group, with

a mug of tea for the driver: 'I brought you a mug of tea: how are you fixed for change for a ten pound note?'

The driver had trouble re-focussing on Arthur: 'Sorry, pal, I've just had to change a note.'

Arthur's grip on the mug stayed firm.

'It so happens,' said Harpo, 'I can oblige you: I have ten pounds sterling in loose change about me even as I speak, less thirty-five p.'

'I can trust you for thirty-five p,' said Arthur. 'Want this mug of tea? It's going.'

The driver was beginning to take on a look of a man going round backwards on a fairground horse.

'I was telling you about the dog.'

'Beg pardon?' said Arthur, who panics easily. 'Is he talking to me? I've got to be back in the shop.' He grasped handfuls of ten pences. 'You been at the meter?'

'Knock knock,' said Harpo.

'Who's there?' The words jerked out of Arthur.

Harpo was at the bus shelter again: 'No answer. *But*, cup and saucer now cleared from glass-topped table. Beetle round to side door.' Action replay, Charlie Chaplin wouldn't have been ashamed. Harpo exploded, tea splattering the company. 'Aaah! Small airborne dog! I scuttered back round out of the way of the outrageous beast, and there, at the front door, this gi-normous miner with cropped hair and steel-tipped boots, all blue scars and malice propense, siezes me.' Harpo hoisted himself by his jacket front, eyes bright with terror. 'Your dog's torn my trousers! I screamed. Would you like to buy a first-aid box on easy terms? Get the hell out of here, he says, I've had about a bellyful of you vultures. Doogle was most pleased with the little scene, said it resembled "High Noon" only faster.'

Arthur licked his lips, looking from face to face.

'This bus is going,' said the driver. 'Don't say I didn't

tell you.' As the door thudded closed, I heard: 'Bleeding grass-eaters.'

'I had a ticket for that bus,' I said.

'They've no consideration,' said Harpo. 'Look what he did to me. And he's late out.'

LOCAL FUNERAL

The church was going to be crowded, so we drew cards for who was to sit next to Harpo's suit, aces low. I don't altogether know why he chose to wear it; he can look perfectly well turned-out in his casuals, he isn't family, so all he needed to do was borrow a black tie. Since it was once Jimmy's suit, perhaps in the back of his mind he wanted to show respect for the dead.

It had been a good suit in its day, but Jimmy was a powerful six foot four, Harpo is five ten and wiry. Also, when the crotch collapsed, it had hung among mothballs and lavender bags for twelve years. Then it went into the lean-to for possible use in the garden for really mucky jobs. But it remained unmistakeably a best suit, it just wouldn't do: a pin-stripe double-breasted three-piece doesn't look right with muddy boots and a shovel.

Harpo had been after a lettuce: 'Good heavens, what an extremely smart suit to be hanging in a garden shed,' he said.

'Take it,' said Bessie. She can be brisk, and once Harpo has embarked on an enthusiasm he finds it hard to get off: the smell went into the same compartment of his mind with the flaws in the double-glazing he sells, the inconvenient Facts Dump, quite close to the gas bill.

Jimmy Medlar on his death-bed had the prone grandeur of a fallen Egyptian statue. The massive arched nose tilted to the ceiling, nostrils flared and showing purple, the eyes now sunken and dark in their sockets, though I knew them to be pale blue, the great jowls seamed with pain, the white sheets straightened with fastidious love by Bessie for my visit.

I suppose he must have done a wrong thing in his sixty-seven years: he paid a drab half a crown for ten minutes through the railings of Wellington Barracks when the Guards were confined to quarters during the General Strike: 'Poor soul, it can't have been much for her.'

He was certainly a fussy man, and could upset Bessie badly over some minor or even imagined neglect of housework. The TV repair man moved the set to look at the back, and made casual conversation as he fiddled: 'D'you live on your own here, then?' Jimmy thought the man saw the dust, created inevitably by the TV static, as evidence of a bachelor's self-neglect, and reproached Bessie, bringing her to tears. A small and double unfairness, since both were obsessively clean and tidy about the house.

That's about all the severest recording angel could chalk against Jimmy's good name.

We made Harpo walk round the cricket pitch for forty minutes before opening time, but he cleared the snug just for walking in: lavender, mothballs, and creosote, combining to make up a dank and wounding whiff of the tomb. There's an iron-on tape you can use to alter trousers and repair, and he'd done a goodish job; the trousers a bit cylindrical where he'd taken off six inches, the crotch stiffened, convoluted and protuberant like a cow elephant's end parts, but the shoulders were excellent. I suppose the heat of the ironing in his tiny kitchen had blunted his sense of smell. We put beermats over our pints.

'I shall be requiring a lift to church from one of you motorized gentlemen,' said Harpo.

I asked the landlord for the cards.

'I'm not having that in my car,' said Clingfilm.

'You could draw cards for that as well,' said Harpo.

Jimmy's two daughters, Angela and Helen, got his measure at fourteen and twelve respectively. I came up Pin Lane from the bus to see him in the garden, rigid with suppressed indignation, hissing up at the bedroom window: 'Angela, Helen, I want this door open at *once*.' Two small faces gazed down impassive, held it as I walked past – I thought it better not to be seen to be watching too obviously – and just before I'd lost them from the periphery of my vision, I caught the simultaneous, brief and dismissive shake of two sets of golden curls.

He was over forty when Angie, the eldest, was born. His first wife departed, full of gin, after a subaltern in the Africa Rifles in the harum scarum of wartime Mombasa. He worked on the railway there, as a fireman, and was no competition for the Sam Browne belt and the overseas allowance of a serving officer. Bessie and he met on a home leave. She came to the village as housekeeper to the doctor, and her unquestioning devotion to duty paralleled Jimmy's – it never seems to have crossed either of their minds that his fund of stories of the daftness and casual indifference of his betters was a kind of philosophy.

They courted quietly but without disguising their love from others. Some were convinced Jimmy would never reappear, and overseas mail was uncertain at the time; Bessie had reason to be grateful for gifts of cot, blankets, nappies, even food, from neighbours. Jimmy came back all the same, and they were married when his wife had divorced him, for desertion.

Bessie looked into the room: 'Is he sleeping? Don't stay if he's tired; I'm glad for him to sleep, and so's he, he's had some dreadful pain.'

'He's promised to say when it's time for me to go.'

Their marriage was muscled by a strong and clear division of labour. Shopping, Jimmy carried the bags. When he was entirely loaded with carriers, and Bessie wanted to see if there was anything else, Jimmy went into the Wine Lodge, lit a very large cigar, got himself a dock of Australian wine and sat, dignified, straight-backed, to watch the old age pensioners trot in, pulling out a clean note to pay and then, anxious not to spill it, or to miss a second of the weekly treat, take a sip at the bar before finding themselves a seat. A pensioner himself, the first shudder which shook their old frames gave Jimmy unfailing delight.

His parched lips moved, he was rehearsing old tales: 'I'd see this lady almost every week, very cleanly and most neatly attired, trotting in opening her purse, eager for her first glass of Guinness of the week, a picture. I said, "Madam, although we've never had any conversation, I've seen you many times in here. It so happens that today is my birthday: I wonder if you'll do me the honour of allowing me to buy you your first Guinness?" "I know what you dirty buggers are after," she said. Nothing was further from my thoughts, Henry, I promise you; may I never move from this spot.'

I knew all the tales: the departure of some friends, to distant places or into death, can be desolating, leaving unpluggable gaps; Jimmy's leaving was rich.

Clingfilm got out of his car and slammed the door, sharp. 'It's no use trying to open that door without a key, it's childproof.' Harpo stared out, a reproachful waif. 'You can bloody stay there till the service is over, you're totally bloody anti-social.' He turned to me: 'It's unbearable in there, un-bloody-bearable; by the *cringe*.'

'He can climb over from the back, can't he? Open a front door?'

'By the time the dumkopf's figured that out, we shall be *seated*, at the end of a pew, which is otherwise *full*.'

'You can't do that to Jimmy's family, be like setting a polecat loose; we owe it to them to form a *cordon sanitaire*. Anyway, have you thought how that smell'll hang about the upholstery?'

Cling unlocked the passenger door. 'Out, this instant. I've got some spray in the glove compartment, we'll try that. It beat the kipper.'

We led Harpo round the back of the church, out of the wind and the public eye.

Cling held Harpo at arm's length, squirting and sneezing: 'I know I drew the low card, but this is the far-side of a joke.'

Alf Cornice's head appeared above the edge of the grave, pale, slablike, monumental as his trade: 'Is that any good for greenfly? I'm plagued with 'em.'

'Blight,' said Cling, teeth gritted, 'Brewer's Blight, it sets like rock.'

'Does it?' said Harpo.

'Well it does on the wife's hair.'

'Hey, I've got to get out of this suit some day you know.'

'You never said a truer word. Come on, into church, I'm beginning to fancy you.'

'Nay you don't want to marry me do you?'

'Shut up, you rednosed clown.'

Jimmy opened his eyes, bright. 'There was some good little perks to being a guardsman those days, Henry.' He was talking about between the wars, he'd been a regular. 'You'd get detailed to man the butts at these public schools. Young cadets training for officers. Get a target without a trace of a hit. Take a pencil and punch a few holes for the lad. ''That's a bit better this week, eh, soldier?'' He'd say, ''Here's ten shillings for yourself; I

59

shall show this to the old man, he thinks I'm a duffer.'' They were toffs, those lads, no doubt. Always saw you right.'

There was something else, something *else*; he talked about Rhodesia for a while, but his voice grew quiet, too quiet to catch.

In church, I could read Jack Ledbury's reaction to the sweet miasma as it crept round him from behind; his neck, creased and waxy, stretched and contracted with thoughts of Eastern promise. Old ram. He craned round, hoody-eyed, to look back at our pew, packed shoulder to shoulder with respectable black. He eased round again to the front, thoughtful. The full aftertaste of creosote, dank mothball and mouldering lavender gripped him; his head swivelled, a sudden glimpse of widened eyes, a sharp cry suppressed as the neckbones crunched, his whisper an incredulous gasp: 'Which of you is it?'

'Him.'

'I might have known it, get him throttled, it'll be a merciful release. My word, I wouldn't keep a hen in that condition.'

I walked back from church. Cling took Harpo home, with all the windows of the car open. We got a promise from Harpo that he'd bin the suit, and in return I would bring round a jar of home-brewed wine to sup Jimmy down. There was unfinished business in my mind, and I thought Harpo would help out. We went over the story of the huge spider on the footplate in East Africa, which Jimmy scooped up with his shovel and threw on top of the wood in the firebox. 'Ten inches across, without a word of a lie, may I never move from this spot.'

Harpo, a first-class story-teller himself, has a passion for the spider one, and does an optional extra impersonation of Jimmy's end-piece: on re-opening the firebox to fill again, the spider is still there, raising one foot after the other in turn ... Harpo blows delicately on the tips of his fingers one by one. 'Ph ... Ph ... Ph ...'

'Harpo, I sat with Jimmy a bit at the end. He was telling me about the Rhodesian Defence Force ...'

'Oh yes, excellent, where they asked them if they'd like to buy their own ammunition to defend the whole of Africa against the Italians in case they came millions of miles south. I'm extremely fond of that one too. Jimmy was deeply patriotic you know.'

'It was about the cavalry officer who came to drill them, right out in the scrub, six hundred miles from the nearest horse: "Shun!" he shouts. "Prepare to mount ... Mount!" No horses, not even a bridle to give you the feel of it a bit. Not a word of a lie. And one man flat on his face in the dust. "What's the matter with you, soldier?" "Bit of trouble with the stirrup, sir." But there was something else? What was he going to say? That's all there is to that story, isn't it?'

Harpo's big spaniel eyes drowned in tears for a moment: 'Well, you know how he always ends his stories, don't you?'

I puzzled at it.

Harpo blew his nose. 'You'll have to excuse me, gentlemen, I'm extremely sentimental about certain things.'

'Well, come on?'

'Used to say, "May I never move from this spot," didn't he?'

BOWLS HANDICAP

Author's Footnote: The game of bowls, as played in Ravensgill, is on a 'green', an expanse of fine grass raised towards the middle to form a 'crown'; the player tries to roll at least one of his two 'woods' (bowls) nearer to the 'block' (a smaller bowl) than his opponent. The woods are slightly biased in shape, so that they can be made to curve across the green, or to run straight against the crown, according to how you bowl.

It's roughly similar to the game Sir Francis Drake played while waiting for the Armada to invade England. The Spaniards, being hidalgos, waited for Sir Francis to finish his 'end' (game); God then sent a wind to scatter England's enemies. This can happen in Ravensgill on a still day: the nodules and subtle irregularities in the ancient turf, known only to experienced locals, can bring dark despair to visiting teams.

One reason this is called a footnote is to give a feel of the bafflement of bowls, another is that when someone's game crosses yours, and may interfere with the progress of your wood, you shout 'Feet!' and the man will leap into the air to let your wood by; it's a part of the mystery of the game that only the person whose feet are in the way leaps.

From our green you look out over the misted sweep of the Pennine Hills, and a tumble of stone-flagged and blue-slated roofs; and Fitchet, as often as he can, looks out over the green: it's his Valhalla. His summers, from windswept Easter Saturday to the rainlashed October handicap, are spent in a fevered dream of happiness, his winters in restless gloom. It was an error for him to take over the job of club steward: the job keeps him near his beloved green, but opening hours prevent him (sometimes) from playing bowls. At such times he peers out from behind the bar, oblivious of customers and duty, following the course of other men's woods with little skips and subdued yelps of encouragement or disgust.

I paused by the green on my way home from taking the children to school; he scurried over to the rail, his little nut-brown Punchinello face eager as a boy's: 'Having a game?'

'I've got a day's work to do, me.'

On the car-park above the green, a young man, with a bowls case; Fitchet's restless eye found him like radar: 'D'you play this game?'

A man carrying a bowls case at 9 am bespeaks a Panel bowler, a professional. I tarried. He was thin, even scrawny, sallow, a heavy brow, boot-nosed, sombre, contained. 'I'm playing in the Area Knockout Saturday, I wondered if I could try the green.'

Fitchet's first wood was a good six feet behind: 'Good road, that, just short of a bit of power.'

The visitor followed the first wood's road within a millimetre; his bowl curved neatly over the crown, described a shallow 'S', passed the block six feet wide, and disappeared into the gutter. As I left about my business, Fitchet was explaining to his new friend, who stood pole-axed, that there was a bit of moss to the right of the crown, a gulley just on from there, and it drops away very sharp at the corner, especially on a dry day.

I wouldn't mind if he was any good of a bowler: his

handicap in the President's Cup is something like eleven, but his advice and encouragement are freely given and in excited and persistent tones. A particularly raggedy end had the contestants calling for 'pegs', the tape for measuring the distances between dubious woods and the block.

'Nay, you don't need pegs for them!' he called from the terrace, 'Run it, and we'll time you!'

Ephraim Boot left the game and climbed the terrace. In his pomp, Ephraim played Rugby League Football for Ravensgill, and in a blood-drenched game against a Roman Catholic Seminary from Yorkshire, it was explained to him at half time that we were thirteen points down due to a jesuitical interpretation of the rules by the brothers and the Abbot, who was referee. It hadn't occurred to Ephraim that forgiveness of sins could be applied to football, but in the second half, enlightened, he helped their scrum-half towards lifelong sexual purity, and assured a golden future in the Church for the full-back, leaving him with a convincing limp and a saintly upwards twist to his neck.

Ephraim's huge white paws closed round Fitchet's middle; Fitchet rose from the ground, squawking like a Rhode Island hen. A small patter of sporting applause, and Ephraim had returned to his game before Fitchet's lungs could find air again: 'Where's your sense of humour, Ephraim? Huh.'

At eleven thirty, I take the dogs out. I should have known he'd still be at it. The visitor's whole frame had a look of knotted determination by now, and he was breathing rapid and shallow to calm himself. 'They call this Fitchet's Channel: no matter how you peg, the wood goes straight, there's a drain underneath.'

The block was with the visitor, and went out, as promised, perfectly straight, the length of the green. His

65

wood followed, slightly wider to allow for the extra weight and increased bias; it settled into the line, suddenly curved round the block, shaving it, and carried on another four feet before collapsing on its side.

Fitchet beamed up at me as he took his place to bowl: 'He's having a hard time this lad, on this green. I'm teaching him all I know, but we've just had a new one, even on me. Must be where Arnold spilled the fertilizer, it's gone bald.' The visitor's lips drew back from his teeth, his eyes staring, maddened. 'He's got a sense of humour, though. Fancy a game?'

Three forty-five, the children erupt out of school like manic confetti; having loved Jesus most of the day, they come out ready to kill. I met them. On the green, the visitor had a homicidal look about him too, wiping his woods with a cloth as if they were missiles.

'Are you going for the record?' I said.

'What?' said Fitchet. 'We've had some good games, me and this lad. He had some sandwiches, that was handy.' The phone rang in the Club.

'Dad, that man's shaking, why is that man shaking? Dad?' I answered the phone.

'It's your wife, Fitchet.'

'What?'

'Jean wants to speak to you.'

He struck his forehead a vigorous blow with his knuckles and stared round as a man waking from a hundred years' sleep. 'The Co-op'll be closed,' he said.

'Nearly four hours ago,' I said.

'What am I going to tell her? You take it.'

'I just did.'

We could see him at the phone in the lobby, jabbing out his free hand and protesting his good intentions: he'd forgotten the shopping, it was half-day closing. The receiver vibrated with Jean's indignation. Nothing for tea.

He has a busy rotatory walk, like a man riding an invisible bike; you don't notice it so much when he's chasing a failed wood across the green, stamping it on into impossible efforts, but loping out of the Club lobby, he had our attention.

'That man's sweating from talking on the phone.'

'Right,' he said, 'who won that end? My block is it?'

'What did she say?'

'What? Oh, the wife; it's definitely a divorce job this time. What can I do? Everywhere's closed. I said to her, I said what can I do?'

'Did she tell you?'

'What? Oh, she said it wasn't up to her, but a box of chocolates occasionally wouldn't come amiss. Me to went is it?'

'Aren't you going to get her some chocolates?'

'What? Oh. Well, what can I do? Everywhere's closed.'

'They sell chocolate at the Shanter, side window.'

'Do they? Oh.' One of the older boys was footling by the green; Fitchet gave him 10p, told him to bring a bar of chocolate from the Shanter and he could keep the change. 'Right, are we bowling or not?'

The day of the finals of the Oldham and District Individual, I watched him, absently thrusting glasses into the 'hedgehog', a machine with rubber brushes which swills and washes, his mind entirely absorbed in the last game. Some customers waited in vain to be served. Linda Buckley was taking round the name-card and a pint pot for the money. That done, she set to and served the thirsty. Then she scratched open the winning name on the card, and looked round for the money: 'There was a potful of pound notes and change on this bar,' she said, crisp.

'What? Was there? I haven't seen it. Kelvin's having

a good game, you know, good bowler.'

'Where's the flaming name-card money, you nut-meg?'

Barry Ogden was looking down into the hedgehog, where pound notes circulated, disintegrating as they went: 'I think I know where your name-card money is, Linda.'

'What?' said Fitchet. 'I've got ten bob on Kelvin, you know.'

The long Tuesday drew towards an unavoidable conclusion. I had a committee meeting, but I couldn't resist finding out. Fitchet stood on the green, his happy face halo'd by the setting sun, the fluffy colourless hair made golden. The stranger was walking with leaden tread up the steps to the car-park.

'Who won?'

'What? Oh, he did; good player. I nearly had him in the slow corner, though; he was amazed when his wood stopped dead in the puddle; he'll know where he is Saturday.'

The stranger stopped and spun to look back, the words wrenched from deep anguish, like a poodle's yap: 'You're as barmy as this naffin' green!'

'I think I might be! Right, thanks for the games, mate. Oh my God, I was going to get the wife a bar of choco-late.'

'You did!' yelped the stranger, bloodshot.

'I did? Who's had it?'

'You put it in your back trousers pocket!'

'Oh Christ, oh, thanks, mate. She thinks the world of me, must do, the things she has to put up with. There'll be nothing for tea, you know, I could have another game.' The stranger glanced down at his bowls case as if it were a thing contaminated, clenched and un-clenched his fingers, wordless, and went.

Fitchet stowed his bowls in the hut, and trotted towards home in the darkening day. He drew out the bar of chocolate, curved by the heat of his bum, stuck with bus tickets and half-smoked cigarettes, and a pound note, which he sucked clean as he went. He waved the sickle of chocolate, the glittering peppermint drooping from its ends like some strange bleached fungus: 'She'll be pleased I remembered her, eh? It's the thought that counts. She's got a wonderful sense of humour, must have, to put up with me.'

A STRANGER

The matron held the new fathers back, kept them milling
and shuffling on the landing outside the maternity
ward, until the minute hand of the wall-clock clicked up
to seven o'clock, her eyes gleaming with amused malice,
her one-piece bosom gripped over folded arms. A queen
bee. He threaded his way through to the pre-delivery
room, found his wife on a grey blanket, on a grey bed,
in a grey, shadowy room; ante-room to light, clean linen,
bright metal, a tilted mirror above to turn the world over
and look at it again. In between contractions, she was
glad for him to be there; during them, she was mostly
too busy, swept by the fierce demands of her belly-
muscles. Adrift in a tidal event, he held on to her hand,
glad in his turn to be able to seem useful. He timed the
spasms for the nurse: three minutes, two minutes fifty
seconds . . .

At eight, he was told to leave by busy women who
came about his wife. He couldn't tell which one spoke,
even how many there were: they had a purpose, he had
none. The clatter of steel dishes, and clacking heels
along the corridors, the waxen, inert people, passing,
fast, on trollies, made him feel like an intruder, an out-
sider to others' troubles . . . X-Ray Dept . . . S1, S2,
Casualty . . . Was this the way he came in? A labourer,
still in his clay-crusted donkey-jacket, sat in an alcove of
curtains, holding a pad of lint stained vivid scarlet to his
nostrils; a neat brown doctor tried to straighten the nose,

71

stepping back each time to judge the effect of the latest twist; the labourer roaring like a bereft cow.

The matron paused on her way, looked in. 'Heavens what a fuss; I've got women having babies and making less noise about it.'

The labourer peered round the white coat of the doctor, pink eyes awash with tears, roared with re-doubled volume: 'Have you ever tried putting one back in?'

She took it out on the husband: 'What do *you* want?'

'My wife's having a baby.'

'Not in here she isn't. Be off with you. Now.'

He found the street, but still didn't rightly know where he was. Went to a coffee-stall. Stand a while, get his bearings. The tea was both brackish and grey, a feeble insult.

'Do youse mind if I have some conversation with ye?'

The man was short, square-built, black hair brushed straight back and greased, deep furrows between cheek-bone and jaw. Dirty shirt crumpled at the collar, dark shiny suit, tight-buttoned, shoes scuffed. He sounded his S's like a Glaswegian. 'Is thish tea no pish?'

He said he'd had TB. Tomorrow was the last test. They would take a great long needle, and push it down behind his collarbone, draw off some fluid, and they would test it. They said he was clear, cured, but he had to go for this last test. To be sure. He didn't want to go to his home, he'd walk the streets. He wouldn't sleep if he went home, for worrying about the morning.

A radiant image in the husband's mind: his nephew on his sister-in-law's round arm. The first new-born baby he'd ever seen, a purple, battered old man with dark matted hair. The mother looked new, not the baby.

'My room's very gloomy, it depresses my spirits.'

He didn't seem greatly troubled, not by the look of his

face; the eyes were sharp on the other's, dark, big pupils, a street-arab's watchfulness in a grown man. The husband puzzled at an indefinable discomfort, set it aside, spoke, offhand; he told the man his wife was in hospital to have their first baby. The man said that was great, really great, they must take a dram together. Was he supposed to do that? Before the test? No, but it beat walking the streets. A four-lane road, with wide pavements, crossing a massive stone bridge over a dark gulf meshed by overhead cables, an expanse of railway lines gleaming below; and somehow, perched in the parapet, a one-room beerhouse, the Sultan. The barman stared over his head as he drew the beers, the other two customers silent. It was as desolate as the road outside; he soon swallowed a pint, and edged out towards the door.

'I'll walk along with ye.'

'What for?'

The man was too close, there would be a foolish confusion as to who was going first.

'I told ye, I'm going to walk the streets; it'll be company for me; I'll keep you company.'

In that huge city, a baby was coming to its birth, their baby; he wanted his mind to be with her mind, clear, willing it to be a sound creature. The man walked by him still, a shadow like his own shadow, a little behind. Get out of my mind.

'I don't need company.'

'Everybody needs company; solitude drives a man to madness.' They passed the house where the man lived. Four-storey, Victorian, flaking blackened stucco, a grimy hand-printed notice in the large window by the door: 'Rooms'. A pale trace of light at the fanlight, all the other windows dark, the woodwork almost paintless. He wished the husband could see the room that he had, it was a terrible place; but walking along at night is interesting is it not? Ye see some things ... He talked about the tramps that sleep in cardboard boxes; you'd be walking along, the street quiet, and a pile of big boxes set out by the shop assistants for the binmen; and one of the boxes moves, just a wee bit, and a foot, shiny with the dirt, raggedy sock on it, comes out, and then gets pulled back in again. Was that not eerie?

He'd worked nights, in a city cafeteria. Washed plates came by on a conveyor belt, out of a machine, and you'd to polish them dry. Three pound a shift. You waited outside the staff entrance, by the loading bay, among the dustbins, and they opened the door at midnight, and the first half dozen got the work. It was warm in there. One time he'd met a man from Motherwell, heard his lingo and said was he not from Motherwell? He was from Glasgow himself. No more than that, just a few words, and there was this great towering pile of plates on the conveyor, all piling up, ahint of him. Wheesht. No man could have held them. They wouldn't even pay him the bit shift he'd worked. You could go again, mind, they didn't know you from before.

They reached the husband's home, and he bade the man goodnight. The man would just come in for a bit; sit till he was ready for his bed; rest his feet a while; maybe a decent cup of tea, eh?

'No.'

Avoiding the other's eye, body stiffened and hunched. The orange light of a streetlamp striking directly down to shadow the man's face; he supposed his own was as blank, unreadable. The faint noise of the other shifting his feet slightly. Cars passing, one, two. It was like turning away from a beggar, the dialogue in your head as you pass by the cupped, outstretched hand.

He couldn't go to his room, he wouldn't sleep, not in

that place. He couldn't eat for what was in his mind, three days, an empty belly churns all night.

'You've got to eat.' The husband was struck by his own vehemence. He had some pig's trotters cooked, with split peas. The man nodded in vigorous agreement, followed him up the stairs. My word this is a fine place, you should see mine's. They'd painted and decorated just, impelled by the coming baby. There was a remaindered carpet on the floor, bought cheap, remaindered because it was self-coloured, a dark orange, the little bed-sitting-room glowed with it, and the old gas fire had new mantles.

The man wouldn't eat, he'd just as soon sit and watch. He liked to see a man eat hearty. It looked good, that food, nourishing. He started to unlace his shoes. The other ate, watching. At a little table in the room, his eye on the man; he wanted to phone the hospital, but the phone was downstairs in the hall. The fork stopped between plate and mouth; he held his breath, and then spoke, forcing a casual tone.

'What are you taking your shoes off for?'

'I don't want to soil this fine carpet you've got.'

'Don't bother your head.'

'I do bother, that's me.'

'You put your shoes on, mister. Now.'

'I thought maybe I'd just kip down here. Anywheres. In a chair maybe. I won't disturb you.'

'You're going home.'

Phone at eleven, the sister had said. Was it eleven? Nearly. He wrestled with the presence of the other. You shake hands, it declares truce. Someone is in your home, it's your bounden duty to make them welcome. You offer food . . . what happens after that? Ancient customs, inborn, snagged. Cut off the stranger from his *right*.

'You'll need to walk with me, for the sake of your

75

company the whiles; it's been great for me, you don't know what it's meant.'

He insisted the husband come in to see the room. A quarter of what had been a spacious first-floor sitting-room; large marble fireplace now hard against the party wall, huge cupboard built into the remaining alcove. Most of the room filled with an iron-framed double bed, a bare twenty-four inches to move about in. A hand-basin. A gas-ring, pink with ancient use and wear. All the furnishings, drapes, bedcover, were discernibly grey, but the overhead gaslight gave a greenish tinge. A room for wretched, sweat-making dreams. The husband escaped, chilled, embarrassed, the man following down the echoing stairs, clomp clomp, clatter.

'I'll walk along with ye.'

'Suit yourself, but you're not coming into the house.' A twist of smile on his face, half turned to the other. 'I take your point, you live in a dump, but that's not my doing. I'm not toting you round for the rest of my life; make me feel like Marley's Ghost.'

'It's just for the company, d'ye see?'

As they parted, outside the house, the man thrust his hand into his jacket pocket, pulled out a spoon, held it out. 'A wee spoon. Ye'll be needing a wee spoon for feeding your baby. Take it.'

He took it ungraciously, to get rid of the man; pocketed it without looking at it. 'Thank you very much.'

Ordinary exchanges, made wrong; he'd wash it straight away. He phoned the hospital as soon as he got in. It was the matron.

'Yes, your wife had a fine baby boy, at eight o'clock this evening; both doing well.'

'How d'you mean? I was with her at eight o'clock.'

'No you weren't. We don't have fathers at the birth here.'

'I think someone should tell you what's going on at your hospital.' He rang off, before she could get the last word in, he knew it'd be good and final; whatever she thought, that tiny boy was at least partly his, he didn't want the quiet bubbles of his happiness punctured.

The baby grew to be a child, to walk, crowing with delight, to talk even. 'We'll never be just the two of us again,' his wife had said. There were bad times, frightening: he drove a tooth through his lip, falling against an iron rail; tottered and tumbled to strike his head on a flagged yard, a resounding skull-crack you could hear two floors up, the yells and grief gone by the time they'd run downstairs; but always they remembered the baby lying, fed and changed, on the big bed, and lying with him to feast on his fine-curled golden hair, the perfect round of head and jaw-line, the set of the small shoulders, the hand that gripped your finger, and squinted at it before dismissing it, the round eyes as he tasted cocoa for the first time, ever.

The husband stood in his local pub.

'I came by to say thanks to ye.'

The man was a stranger. Black hair greased back, crumpled collar of shirt escaping from a dark shiny suit, tight-buttoned. The scuffed shoes were a clue.

'Do I know you?'

'Ye kept me company at a very bad time in my life: I was recovering from the TB. I remembered you saying this was your local, so I came by.'

'It's my local. When did I say that?'

'That's my local, you said, as we walked by. I took your advice, d'you know.'

'What the hell advice was that?'

He remembered him now. He remembered the man, hour upon hour, walking, chatting, dogged, but he remembered nothing of what had been said; he remembered the spoon, lying among spare cutlery in the kitchen drawer, never used, on the handle, stamped in flowing letters: 'Lyons'. He hadn't said anything of consequence had he? He didn't know what that evening had been about, but it hadn't been anything to do with words. *Advice?* He felt hollow. To reject another person is to reject a part of yourself, in the sense that you know how the other feels, very clearly, it's shared; you don't like what you find in yourself, you feel as empty as the other, you face a wall.

'I never gave you any advice.'

'I saw your nice home, and I thought, that's nice, I could do with something the likes of that. She's a widow, with a bit house of her own. Just a few rooms. We let them out, to fellers that needs it. I do the administration. It's a small income, d'you see? And I've got company. D'ye see that? Will ye take a dram with me?'

TWICE-NIGHTLY, THURSDAY OFF TO LEARN IT

Before settling here among the hills, I was a peripatetic actor; still am, come to think of it. As often as work, or being out of work, would allow, I came to walk, to breathe air that had not been breathed before, and hear the grouse rattle off. My day-by-day prospect was not so grand.

We were playing *Cyrano de Bergerac*, twice-nightly. I was supposed to be a bold swordsman.

'I like your frock,' said Ray. 'I'll lend you some of my bangles.' Stage manager of the Theatre Royal, he didn't look all that dashing himself, dressed as a seventeenth-century pastrycook, big floppy white hat, flowing apron down to his ankles, his thick make-up a mask suggesting maybe a chubby Claudette Colbert.

I was assistant stage manager, small parts as cast, must have lounge suit, sports jacket, evening dress or dinner suit, four pounds ten shillings a week. The director was a slim-built man, with a boyish, slightly nasal voice; an excellent light comedian, he had chosen to play and direct himself as the rugged, quarrelsome, golden-voiced Cyrano, with the kind of doomed enthusiasm that convinces rich businessmen of a certain age that they can conduct symphony orchestras. He always wore a wide-brimmed felt hat, and if he got excited in rehearsals, he would raise it slightly with both hands, turn it full circle, and settle it back into place. I'd have done anything for that director.

'We're doing *Brighton Rock* next week,' he said. 'We shall need a coffin and a telephone box. Get on to the GPO.'

All props and furniture were borrowed, free, 'for the advert'. I once borrowed the large roller from the Parks and Gardens, to rumble across slats nailed to the floor backstage, for the train effect in *Ghost Train*. The depot is at the top of the town, the theatre at the bottom; I clanged downhill with the wind whistling in my burning ears, hurtled across traffic lights at red, past unbelieving policemen on point duty, wondering whether I'd make it round the corner into the market, and how was I going to *stop* it? The woman whose stall I used as longstop was surprisingly unruffled: 'It's all seconds anyway,' she said.

There was a long, stunned pause when I asked the GPO engineer for the loan of a phone box; then he said: 'Have you any idea how much these things *weigh*?'

Something like two tons, as I recollect. The director stared down at the ancient scored boards of the stage floor, brooding, and finally opted blithely for a wooden mock-up. The carpenter went out to the Swan and got amazingly drunk. I got the coffin. 'A coffin? For a week? Theatre Royal? I don't think that presents any problem,' said the undertaker. 'Full? Or empty?'

It turned out did I mean with lining or without, but I measured my reply carefully.

The Equity Minimum Wage for twice-nightly was slightly higher than for once, to compensate for the hours. I never saw it. 10 am to 10 pm, six days a week, Saturday night to Sunday morning to strike and re-set for the next show, Thursday off to learn it. When we did *The Love of Four Colonels*, I spent the evening moving furniture and props on and setting for the following scene, striking and stacking the previous one, and then round the back to be ready to bring on for second house. I was toiling in the gloom of backstage, when suddenly the working lights came on; Ray stared at me in the pale dusty light: 'What d'you think you're doing?'

'Setting for second house,' I said.

'That *was* second house,' he said.

Actors would accept a job, get off the London train, see a bill advertising twice-nightly, and get straight on the next train back. An actress was due on a Monday to rehearse for the following week, and it was comfortably assumed she would play a walk-on maid that day. We didn't catch a glimpse, she was on her way. The management would have been wiser not to have posters too near the railway station.

A stage-struck programme-seller was recruited to walk on with a large oval tea-tray, place it on a low table, and depart, while light-hearted banter was exchanged by the rest of the cast, creating an atmosphere of leisured money. She was fine at the dress; bit wooden, but she did her job with a shove from me on cue. Her gay showbiz chatter in the Green Room was a tonic. First house, Act Two, the baronial home – we always had three acts, for the bar sales – the massive oaken door flirted loose from its ball-catch: it was her début. I don't know how she came to take hold of the tray sideways, instead of presenting it to the door the narrow way, as rehearsed. The cast became aware that their elegant artifice was being overtaken by an urgent truth, upstage right. Concentrated on her tinkling load, the young actress, and the audience, debated her problem with suppressed hysteria: thirty-inch door hole, thirty-inch tray, plus knuckles.

She tried tilting the tray gingerly: the milk slopped from the silver jug (courtesy of Elton's, fine silver and watch repairs), and lumps of sugar toppled gently. Tried tilting the other way: the teaset slid smartly down and halted in ranks like guardsmen, just in time. She turned and backed in, her charming black-draped rump, with a bow of frothy white apron strings, bucking and sawing as the tray refused the door again, the audience helping each other back on to their seats.

The shadowy, flame-red face of Ray appeared in the doorway; he snatched the tray, thrust it back at her correctly aligned, and slammed the door. Through sweat-streaked wisps of hair, the maid looked round, an expression of mulish panic in her eyes that went clear to the back of the upper circle. She advanced on stilted legs, laid down the tumble of crocks, awash with tea and milk and a grey mud of sugar, strode to the vast open fireplace, ducked under the hood, and disappeared from public view. As far as the audience ever knew, she was still up the chimney at the play's end: she declined to take a curtain call, weeping, even though I assured her that the audience thought her the best thing since Grimaldi.

Cyrano de Bergerac was more serious. I enjoyed fencing, in a slap-happy sort of way, and the company would have sessions, including the director.

'I'll kill you on the balcony,' he said, 'and you can fall backwards.'

I had a word with the scene designer. 'Twelve feet,' he said. 'He wants the rail reinforced with scaffolding for some reason.'

The actors had departed to pubs and digs, the stallholder outside the stage door below called quietly to punctuate the still afternoon: 'Where you like dear ... where you like ...'

I worked on in the prop room, painting foil and sabre guards with black enamel curlicues to give them a period aspect.

The lighting board was above the prompt corner, access by vertical iron ladder to a plank bridge supported by a stout steel scaffold. About twelve feet up. My steps rang on the ladder in the silent theatre, arrows of white sunlight through the cracks in the elephant doors.

'Where you like dear ... where you like ...'

This was for my revered director; I felt like Sydney Carton; a mug. A deep breath. I staggered back, head bowed in death, Cyrano's imaginary blade under my left armpit, the sabre dropping from my nerveless grasp to clatter on the planks. Both hands gripped the rail, and the lighting board and fly gallery revolved over me with the slow pace of a swirling nightmare as I went my full length, arms stretched, before letting go. The steel uprights twanged like a Roman siege catapult, and I arc'd through the air to thud flat to the stage floor, knocking every trace of wind from me. After a rest, I limped back to the Green Room, and continued painting black enamel curlicues with shaking hands.

'I've tried the twelve foot backwards fall,' I told him next day, 'off the lighting bridge.'

'Good,' he said, 'we'll do it when we come to it.'

'I think I may have broken a rib.'

'Oh,' he said, 'might be better to do it off a table.'

'I could do it head-first off a table,' I said.

FIT-UP TOURING, ALSO TO HELP IN KITCHEN

The roar and cough of the ancient engine fell away to silence. Midnight on the low hills above Dundee, the back of the coach crammed with set, props, costume skips, lighting equipment. Tim, electrician and driver, got out to look under the bonnet. We left the fug to stretch our legs and gasp and gulp in the icy November air. Not a star.

We became aware of a faint creaking, as if the black bowl of the sky were one immense ice-pack, moving and grinding, way above our heads. Tim stopped his tinkering and listened with us, his face lit from below by the glow of a tiny hand torch, his deep-sunk eyes and long teeth just slightly demonic: 'Geese,' he said, 'migrating geese.'

Starting coach and wagon engines in winter was always a chore in fit-up touring. I have frozen recollections of taking out sparkplugs, one by one, setting them to heat in a saucer of burning spirit, replacing them, then cranking until the handle threw me in the air like a ragdoll, a few bronchitic chugs, and then back into obstinate, cold silence. Out with the plugs again. For hours. Days even. I suppose I was cheap, and new motors expensive. I didn't mind, the girls were pretty, fresh-faced, not an ounce of flab: we all had jobs. I'd wear gloves for the greasier tasks, but still somehow I'd end up blackened, wondering how much would transfer to the bread-dough I had it in mind to bake later.

We were taking live theatre to the people. Arts Council policy changed later, along the lines of the Billington Councillor, when they enquired about Marlene Dietrich's fee to appear at their new Arts Centre, so as to bring people in to get to know it; there was an awed silence when the amount was reported.

'I think mebbes,' said the Councillor, 'we'd be better off asking Miss Dietrich to stay right where she is, and we'll spend the money taking the population of Billington to see her.'

Dial M for Murder, *Dandy Dick*, *The Little Hut*; the last an innocent romp involving a suggestion, never fulfilled, of some small adulterous delight. Local amateurs worked to promote the tours, and helped front of house. One gaunt and tweeded gentleman remarked confidentially, as I staggered past with a portable switchboard, 'I had heard it was rather naughty, so I thought I'll just glance at the first act, and then go to my home. But I quite liked it, so I stayed till the end.'

In Arbroath, the high roaring seas cast a spume that thudded against the back wall, but even that didn't drown the stertorous breathing of a man in the front row.

'Can you hear him?' whispered the leading lady, a curvy young actress with large dark eyes, whose desert island rags would have made saints in their niches stir. 'The man, breathing.'

'Actually that's not a punter,' said Tim, 'it's a Saint Bernard dog that enjoyed the book, so they've brought him along to see the play.'

I'm talking about two different kinds of fit-up here, both with an honourable tradition reaching back into time. One in which you carried scenery etcetera, and played whatever halls you could get . . .

'Can you play hunchback?'

'I suppose so.'

88

'Right, you do the box office, and then play the hunch-back tonight . . .'

And in the other kind, the theatre itself was moveable: long trailers whose sides let down or were lifted to form floor or roof, with separate panels to fill in the side walls. Ours was mechanized, but in the old days they were horse-drawn, with hessian screens for the sides.

Annie belonged to those old days, a Tiggywinkle of a woman, with a foghorn Lancashire accent; I suppose she would have been what they called a 'Utility Woman'. She came to us out of nostalgia, I think, to help us in the kitchen. She wagged her curls over our jerseys, cords, wellies and duffle coats: 'In my day, you never went into town without your full silks and pearls, and a big feather hat: you were a artiste in them days.'

Annie told an apocryphal tale, which had a ring of truth about it for me, of one Archie Leach, who later went on to become a famous Hollywood star. 'The boss always played the hero, see, even when he were getting on a bit, and he always did have a bit of a impediment. And when this young lad came along, of course *he* wanted all the dashing parts, wouldn't entertain nothing else. Well, the boss'd only taken him on as a favour to the lad's father, who couldn't do nothing with him. "You come here, with the arshe out of your britches, demanding this and that; you can get it into your head that in this company *I* play Romeo, and that's flat, or you can get out." And get out he did. Went to America.'

One of the things the two sorts of fit-up had in common was Tim, who at various times was electrician with both. Backstage in Forfar he showed me a row of earthenware pipes, set upright, into which were suspended metal rods.

'Heavens to Betsy,' I said, 'what are they?'

'Dimmers,' he said, his eyes glittering in their sockets.

'As you lower or raise the rods in the water, you alter the resistance, so you get more or less current in the lamps.'

'*Water?*' I said.

He had, besides a devotion to the most terrifying and cockamammy electrical setups, a compendious knowledge of local digs. He found Minnie for me, at whose house I stayed often over the years, sunk in a goosedown mattress, with a fire of miners' concession coal thundering up the chimney. She looked a hundred and two when I first met her, small, stooped, with an ivory complexion like an old apple. Whatever time of day you returned she'd be on her way upstairs with two giant buckets of coal, giving little high grunts as she climbed. I could never convince her I wasn't Henry Irving: 'Hallo, Mr Irving, I've saved you the upstairs front as usual.'

'Livings, Minnie, Henry Livings.'

'Yes, well, I daresay you'll know your way by now, Mr Irving.'

It's all a long time ago, but I have an image now of a hungry chattering company bringing steam, noise, and aching hunger to a tiny Viennese cake shop in the Highlands; thick coats, and strange floor-length mufflers, portable chessboards, the *Manchester Guardian*; Tim's stringy figure in flannels, short-sleeved shirt, a small pullover against the penetrating cold. Why was it always winter in those days? I was the last to arrive; two mature ladies were snapping closed their purses and adjusting Paisley scarves over the collars of Melton coats as they came out. 'It's a vairy nice place,' I heard, 'but you do see some queer people.'

The last time I stayed with Minnie, I had the feeling of being at the end of an era. Her sister-in-law greeted me: 'Hello Mr Irving,' she said, 'come in, it's all right; Minnie's gone.'

'Oh dear, how very sad.'

'Only last week. She said she felt a bit tired, so I said you go and have a lie-down, I'll do the rooms and the fires. Half-past four, no sign of her. I thought I'll take her up a cup of tea. She was laid there, on the bed, looking at me. I said d'you want this cup of tea? She didn't speak. She just turned over, broke wind, and died.'

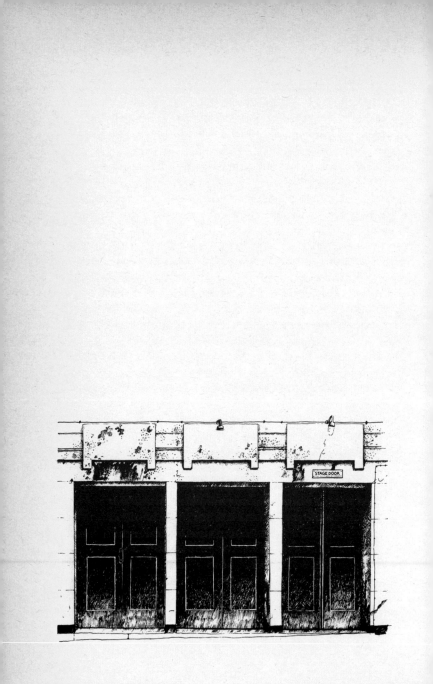

WILL THE DEMON KING PLEASE WEAR THE HAT PROVIDED?

The assembled singers, dancers, speciality acts, comedians and feeds talked earnestly about sticking faithfully to the story, getting it to the kids; Danny, watery-eyed veteran of panto, wiped away a griefless tear and spoke to me as if we were alone: 'Remember all the trouble we had with the Ogre last year? Speciality act with eight bleeding ten-foot dancing giants, UV lighting. We had no chance: Ogre came on like Tweedledee after that lot.'

This year's Ogre was tall, with long mucky fingernails, and dank hair down to his collar; even with a pint of stout he had the air of being ready for Richelieu's Farewell, left hand akimbo, head lifted in noble grief. We had part-scripts, containing just your cue, and then the line: 'dot dot dot see you again: Ahah, but you will see me again my proud young fellermelad!' My script as Demon King was the size of a child's exercise book, my colleague's four sparse pages.

'My word,' he said, 'you do seem to talk a lot.'

He settled to the *Telegraph* crossword, and the rehearsal weeks bustled round him. He may have gone for a costume fitting. They brought my cloak, green tailcoat and strap-under trousers to the rehearsal studio; and the hat, a grey, crumpled soft topper, reminiscent of Micawber. Costumes and scenery descended from spectacular West End blockbusters, year by year, to the provincial number one theatres, finally crumbling in out-of-season resorts and town halls. I guessed my hat was on its fifth circuit.

'The race doesn't always go to the fleet,' said Danny, deadpan. To this day, I couldn't tell you the plot of *Puss in Boots*; I was King Rat one year. Maybe that was *Puss in Boots*. Or else *Dick Whittington*. I remember a fly-man talking fondly and proudly of pantomimes he had worked on. 'We flew this giant clock in, practical clock it was, back-lit; you could see it glowing down there.'

'Cinderella,' I said.

'What?' he said.

We had a horse, an unhappy horse. The front end was normally a goose, a role in which he triumphed, he would explain. Apart from the odd children's party, twelve weeks panto was the most work he got in a year, the rest was washing-up in his brother-in-law's café. He was a wiry, small man, ideally made for crouching for hours inside a skin, and performing impossible contortions, hand up inside the beak, and he was very well paid when he did work. He spent it all, at once, mainly on entertaining the rest of the company long enough to give us a full account of his skills. The diet, mostly curry, and beer, played impressive tricks with his metabolism.

'Did you know there's a left and a right to goose feathers?' I was quite interested the first time he told me. 'Every feather hand-sewn.'

His wife played the back half of the horse with sustained indignation; her hot tousled head thrust out of the zippered escape-hatch, she snarled, nightly: 'Christ, it's not fit to breathe in here.'

The throat-mike Danny ordered for the Ogre, because the huge papier-mâché head made the man's orotund tones indecipherable, was an insult and a bafflement. His amplified enquiry echoed round a sparsely

94

attended matinee during the Principal Girl's 'When You Wish Upon a Star . . .'

'IS IT ON?'

That made the pensioners sit up.

Danny took the comedians' late arrivals at rehearsal calmly, sighed over Puss's delightful but faint singing voice, and made notes about microphones, relayed messages about the hat, laconic: 'They tell me it was created specially for the show.'

One day, a wizened old man, with jet black shiny hair, appeared at the studio door: 'Am I right for *Robin Hood*?'

Danny shambled forward like a respectful chamberlain. 'No, you're upstairs, Jack; *Robin Hood*'s in number four.' He ushered the old man across the room to an inner door, holding his arm gently to guide him. 'Still doing the cat are you? Marvellous.'

'They keep asking me to do it, but I'm too old for it: can't do the twiddly bits any more.'

'Seventy are you by now? Marvellous.'

'Seventy-two.'

'Marvellous; good luck, careful how you go.' Danny closed the door, and turned, irradiated. 'Finest cat in the business. Couple of years ago, I couldn't finish the Ballroom scene; I kept saying to Jack, it's not finishing, this scene, do something Jack. And he'd say, "I'm too old, Danny, can't do the twiddly bits any more." There I am, opening night Southsea, chewing my nails over the Ballroom scene, side of the stage, when I hears this roar like Niragara Falls from front of house; I dashed through the iron door, and there's Jack, way up on the circle rail, miaowing top of his voice, the audience in ecstasies of terror and delight. Right round he goes, down on to the front of the Royal Box, hops on to the stage, bit of a tiddly wiggle of his bum, and off. What an artist!'

We sat silent.

'A table won't stand with three legs,' he added. Rehearsals ground on, the Ogre first to his corner, last to go, speechless. Finally the musical director arrived, a careful, gentlemanly young man, deeply committed to panto: even in rehearsal he hissed me, sotto, for practice. There was a pause.

'It's gone quiet, hasn't it?' said Danny. 'Who's it supposed to be?' He glanced at his master-script: 'Supposed to be the Ogre.'

'Oh, is it me?' He set aside the *Telegraph*, and rose. We stared; he seemed to be putting on size, weight, power, tufted hair: Quasimodo straightened out. 'Fee, fi, fo . . .'

'Wait a minute,' said the MD, 'I think I've got some "Fee fi fo fum" music here.'

My dressing room at Bradford had housed Chipperfield's lions before I moved in. I didn't use it much, but the hat, which never left it, gradually absorbed a rank, mind-stunning leonine stench.

'Management's out front tonight,' said Danny, on a fleeting visit to the show. 'You could wear the hat.'

I got a grip on it. Chorus girls who normally greeted me cheerfully looked round absently, nostrils twitching. 'You should see a doctor,' said the comedian.

Even the back half of the horse stopped in the middle of her embittered commentary. 'He's been eating fish-glue,' she said, with wonder.

The Demon and the Ogre are pretty soon on for the walk-down. The ranks of dancers fan out, arms raised. I bowed with extravagant irony, acknowledging the children's enraged boos; a good night. As I left centre stage, the hat lay on the walk-down steps, right under the Ogre's ponderous boots as he thumped after me, almost sightless in the head, grinding on the hat to turn and lumber to his place in the line-up. The horse followed, in a frisky sideways skitter that buffeted the hat between four hooves. In the silence that accompanies loud noise I heard: 'You'd better be home at a decent time, it's pie and chips.'

Last of all, the loveable comedian sailed down, booting the hat snappishly out from under his glittering ballgown, smiling graciously the while, and scoring a neat goal in the orchestra pit. The MD beamed round, the house roared. After this, it was a hat a night, or no hat.

There was a note on my dressing table. A tear had formed a small dimple on the paper. 'Management says not bother with the hat. See you next year. Danny.' And underneath: 'The man with profit on his mind aims high, but often strikes low.'

SUTCLIFFE – RAMSDEN

We were all looking forward to Mel Tressel's account of the wedding. He'd been invited by Maureen and Geoff to the reception at the Co-op Hall, and he'd promised to get a full report into the *Advertiser*, and a photograph, with the cake. They call him Tango Tressel, on account of the way he moves, his arms swinging as if he were playing two invisible yo-yos. He'd been to the match at Watersheddings during the afternoon; he breezed in, jacket flapping; Maureen moved between him and the cake.

'Good match this afternoon, Geoff,' he said, 'you'll be sorry you missed it, I dare say. Mind, the best team lost.'

I knew for a fact it'd been a draw.

Most of the guests seemed to be there, the hand-shaking was over.

'I've got a photographer to come at eight, when every-body's here,' said Mel, and made for the bar.

'Why does he want everybody here for photographing the cake?' said the bride's mother. 'There'll only be you and Geoff, won't there?'

'Perhaps he thinks it's a pile of pennies,' said Geoff.

Mrs Sutcliffe's goodwill was fragile; her mind went back to the last-minute safety-pin, Maureen's dangling bra, hair in spikes, and the sweat rose under her make-up, warming her face. Geoff and Maureen, arm in arm, moved among the trestle tables, chatting with easy dig-nity to people who'd known them since they were born;

99

he in grey tailcoat, tall, burly, slightly balding at twenty-five, straight as a tree, clenching his motor-mechanic's hands, although he'd scrubbed and bleached away the grime; she in her grandmother's wedding dress, an ivory silk sheath, flounced at the hem, a cloche hat over glossy dark brown hair, framing her rosy cheeks. They looked royal.

Uncle Arnold sat pinched, and a little desperate, fuddled from the afternoon meal at the Shanter. He'd been delegated to Reply for the Guests, and was in sore need of a workable joke. Whatever kind of speech you made at a wedding, there had to be a joke in it; unhappiness like a beehive filled his chest with busy pain. Mrs Tressel sat opposite him, steadily pushing egg and cress bunnies into her mouth from a small piled plate before her, her moustache rising and falling, not good company.

'Hello, mother,' said Mel, sitting down with a flourish of arms and coat-lap. 'Getting plenty to eat, eh?'

I found a place at the next table; conversations with Mel can be confusing, better taken at a distance, it gives you time to figure out where he's got to.

'There was this magistrate's court,' said Arnold.

'It's her age you know,' said Mel, 'she can eat a tater more'n a pig.' Mrs Tressel stared at her son, speechless with bunnies, malevolent.

'I expect it passes the time for them, eh?' said her son.

'There was this magistrate's court. It's a joke.'

'Oh yes?'

'Been a motor accident, young mother and father killed, only survivor, eighteen-month-old child; magistrate wants to find out what happened, child can't talk, see?'

'Terrible, terrible,' said Mel. 'Was this the one on Huddersfield Road, Friday?'

'It's a joke.'

'Of course. You get some shocking accidents on that bad bend.'

'That was a wagon and trailer.'

'I know, I was there shortly afterwards. Thursday. Or else Friday.'

'So the magistrate says to the child, what was Daddy doing at the time of the accident?'

'Only survivor, eh? Phew.'

Arnold raised his voice as his spirits went lower: 'And the child went . . .' Here Arnold made a snoring noise, eyes half-shut, head back.

'Asleep, eh? Asleep at the wheel; I know, it can happen. Police think that may have happened with the wagon and trailer Wednesday.'

'Stuff the wagon and trailer. So the magistrate says to the child, what was Mummy doing at the time of the accident? And the child went . . .' Arnold made like reading a book, turning pages and scanning down at speed.

'Reading a book? Well who was driving the car? That's what I want to know. Some people are completely irresponsible.'

Arnold got up abruptly, walked unseeing down the hall. There's an iron stanchion supporting the balcony. He stood with his forehead against it, his lips working.

The disco had started up, a steady roar, the operator a smirking gargoyle, caged in noise. The older end sat, hammered into silence. A few children ran about, or rolled on the floor. Arnold came back to his chair and sat, violently. He gripped Mel's sleeve: 'Magistrate says to the child, what were *you* doing at the time of the accident?'

Made uneasy by Arnold's bloodshot urgency, Mel made light conversation: 'Mother's on her third plate of bunnies, she likes her bunnies.'

Arnold's voice was hoarse and high, tight in his throat: 'IT DOESN'T MATTER!'

'Oh I know that; all you can eat and more; excellent spread; and Proctor's have done a first-class job on the cake. I've got a photographer coming along, should be here by now.'

'So the child goes, brrrm brrrm brrrm.' Arnold held an imaginary steering wheel before him, eyes popping, lips drawn back from his teeth in a dreadful smile.

Mel produced a notepad and tore off a page, patting it flat on the beer puddles of the table: 'If you could just jot down the main details; I'll confirm it with the police of course. Excuse me.'

Arnold chewed his knuckles, giving off a small animal whimper. Mel swung out of his seat and went off towards the cake, his wide strides and flailing arms carving a way through the dancers, who were beginning to come on to the floor for a quickstep.

It looked theatrical, even balletic; the bright neon glare beneath the balcony emphasized by the shadowy figures on the dance-floor, the sombre pulsing lights of the disco equipment at the opposite end of the hall, orange, purple, yellow. Arnold sat, anchored in deep anxiety, the scene by the cake now clear, now obscured, as the dancers circulated; he made baby bubbles with his lips, bl-bl-bl-bl-bl, sketched the steering-wheel mime; caught my eye, stopped himself, glanced about, furtive.

Mel fussed about Geoff and Maureen, straightening the dress, adjusting Geoff's carnation; the aim was to get the glittering pile of gift-wrapped presents, nests of bright pans, blankets in misty polythene, small cutters for making shell-shapes out of butter, all into the picture. The bride and groom stood either side of the cake, formal, earnest, the lens their master. Ice-white, four-tiered, the cake stood taller on its little table than Geoff. Mel was satisfied, stepped away, the photographer raised his camera. It was a card table, with folding legs, perfectly sturdy with the weight of the cake.

Nobody saw the beginning of it, everybody saw the end. The back of Mel's shoe must have caught under the lower cross-strut of the table, and he must have jerked it loose as he sidled out of the picture. Suddenly the vertical lines were altered, the cake seemed to pause at an angle; Mel grabbed at air like a failed juggler, the porcelain pillars flirting through his hands every which-way, splintering and cracking about the astounded photographer's feet. The top three tiers continued with accelerated momentum, the edge of the table top hit the floor, the bottom tier slid and shattered as if punched by a giant fist.

A trampled snow of icing and battered lumps of dark cake covered the floor and the presents in a wide tri-angle. In the thunder of the Gold and Silver Waltz, Mrs Sutcliffe's small painted mouth circular, and her terrible primal scream rising to the iron trusses of the roof, her top set falling away like a spent rocket-booster to clack down on her bottom teeth as she screamed, on and on, her eyes stretched wide as if astonished by her own noise. Maureen's head jammed into Geoff's shoulder, rigid. A hot, fixed grin on Geoff's face, as if he had a cucumber in there, sideways, his eyes slightly crossed. Arnold bowed slowly to rest his head on the table, his shoulders shuddered uncontrollably, his hand gripped his scalp to make seagulls of his lacquered hair; I bent by him to see his face, wondering if he was ill; the laughter flowed out of him, dotted with hiccups, a honeyed balm. Mrs Tressel had stopped eating.

Mrs Sutcliffe dictated a short announcement on the phone to the *Advertiser*, her voice a miracle of gritted control. Any contribution from Mr Melvin Tressel, and she would sue.

'SUTCLIFFE–MARSDEN
The wedding took place on Saturday at St Mary's
Church Ravensgill of Maureen Sutcliffe, only daughter
of Mr & Mrs James Sutcliffe, to Geoffrey Ramsden, eldest
son of Mr & Mrs Henry Ramsden. One insertion only.'

THE BOY WAS ME

The Blitz lit up Manchester like a rosy torch. In the morning you could walk across Market Street on the plaited firehoses without your feet touching the ground, marvel at the engines from as far away as Glasgow, gaze wonderstruck at the sooty fabric of the gutted Royal Exchange, the Deansgate Hotel, the miraculous survival of one side of the timber-framed Shambles, and the cosy old cathedral, windowless.

Summer 1941, the sky was open. At night, barrage balloons gleamed high against searchlights being tested, or hoping to pinpoint planes in the groaning shoals of Heinkels and Dornier bombers. I know an Englishman who was trapped as a child in wartime Berlin, for whom the banshee wail of air-raid sirens and the gritty drone of English Lancasters and Halifaxes have the same heart-stilling effect even now when we hear them in recordings. Permanently in the memory the thud of the anti-aircraft cannon on the spare ground off St Ann's Road, the flame of the candle in our refuge under the stairs juddering rhythmically in time with the detonations, the sharp crack of a piece of shrapnel hitting the tiles, to be sought out next day and treasured.

There was a very dull, buck-toothed, specky-four-eyed child, about ten at this time. And in that glorious summer, when the tar of the roads bubbled, when a dragon-fly hovered, mysterious and primeval over the dyeworks dam, his parents sent him, and to this day he doesn't believe it, to Southport, to his Grandma's. He and his younger sister stood among the hooting hissing and crash of violent steam engines in Victoria Station, with small suitcases, suddenly benumbed to find it really was happening. After all that had happened, we were back to nothing again.

The reason I say he was dull is he never talked to anyone; he made 'boing' noises into the empty bath, clicked his tongue like castanets as he walked along, but never talked: he couldn't think of anything to say which he imagined might interest anyone, so he shut up. Everyone else was interesting. They had a bike, or a catapult, or great quantities of marbles, but this one had books, which were of interest only to himself. So he watched the others, and kept his counsel. Grownups were mostly a threat. It was a feature of the time that grown people would shake their fists at children and shout obscure and angry remarks. Horny Harry, the Co-op milkman, stood silent and still with a girl among the rhododendrons, and the boy stood as silently to watch. 'Gerrawaywiyer!' shouted Harry, shaking his fist.

I didn't mention the gasmask case. Gasmasks, which we were obliged to carry everywhere, came in stout cardboard boxes. A canvas case could be bought which would sling conveniently over the shoulder, but the boy's father worked on making barrage balloons, and scraps of balloon fabric were easily got, and not too difficult to sew up to make a case, which had the extra advantage of being waterproof, so the cardboard wouldn't get soggy in the rain. That was round his neck, and his sister's, and his mother's, as they stood on platform thirteen, Victoria Station, Manchester, benumbed and unbelieving. Grandma must have had a gasmask too, even babes in arms had them, but she had so many parcels, unwrapped articles like saucepans, and brown paper carrier bags slung about her it was difficult to identify any individual box. She had been a stunning golden-haired country girl in her youth, and was now a small, embattled, overwhelmingly energetic sixty-year-old, a martyr to bunions, but otherwise fit to jump over a table. Recollecting her character, I suppose she could easily have defied the government in the matter of gasmasks, as she defied them with her hoard of jars of molasses, bags of oatmeal, batallions of tinned vegetables and fruit, corned beef and jam. Hoarding was anti-British, but Grandma was strongly pro-Grandma.

Every morning in that sand-invaded house, the two children had oatmeal porridge, molasses, and top of the milk. The sister was mulishly unhappy, she ate little and refused a lot, so her rosy good looks grew pinched; the boy never spoke, so nobody knew whether he was unhappy or not. He drank pee out of a bottle in the garden shed one day. It was an event.

And when the long summer ended, and the myriad chalky snails that mysteriously silvered the dry gritty house walls had hidden themselves against the coming winter, when the bubbles in the tarmac had all been popped by the boy, they went to school, his sister and he, in Southport.

Such was the rapid call-up of young men that there were only half enough teachers, and half the school was permanently on rota community singing in a homely chapel hall. They would walk like refugees in huge crocodiles through the autumn air that smelt of soot, past unknowable buildings along strange empty streets, from the harsh new brick of the school, into the scruffy hall, warm, smelling of hot iron, whose portico he only ever glimpsed from among jostling raincoats. 'Roll Out the Barrel', 'My Old Tarpaulin Jacket', 'Run Rabbit Run ...' Was his sister there? he saw her occasionally at playtime through the railings; she seemed to talk to the other girls. They said 'hallo' to each other.

The other half of the time they were in huge, silent classes; massed, miserable incomprehension. The teacher wasn't particularly a bully. 'If you can't see, sit at the front, runt,' he told the boy. He was certainly less of a tyrant than Miss Wragg had been at primary school, in front of whom small children would wet themselves and the floor with terror.

'There's a smell in here,' he said; he came back to it later: 'Can anybody else smell that smell?' Some could, some couldn't, so he said, 'Settle down, SETTLE DOWN!'

Occasionally, during those first weeks, the teacher would open cupboards and root about, looking for the source of the smell. He looked behind the blackboard, in the waste-paper basket, in his desk drawer, bringing the contents forward gingerly, nostrils aflare. In the children's desks ... The second Friday, he took on the aspect of a tracker dog, concentrated, vigorous, interrupting a geography lesson in mid-sentence. The alteration in subject matter was not at first detected by the boy; the man might as well have been talking in a series of clicks. Any knowledge in the boy's head came from his own books, and they were at home in Manchester, in his bedroom. He didn't connect the noises bawled at him by teachers with communication, nor did he think the noise contained information: it was just a noise.

The teacher was a curly-haired, fair-complexioned young man, straight-backed, keen, but bereft of kindliness as far as the boy could tell; his face swung close to the boy's. 'It's here somewhere, it's somewhere about you. Give me that gasmask case. Good grief, I thought a cat was getting in. You'll have to change that thing; I can't have that in here. Change it dinner time.'

The stench of the warm rubberized fabric reached the boy; his imagination had been fending it off for two weeks, keeping it at waist level. It wasn't his. He hoped it wasn't his.

During 'Oh My Darling Clementine' that afternoon his mind concentrated on how not to come to school with it on the Monday; you had to carry a gasmask, it had to have a case. There wasn't another gasmask case to be had in the whole world. His Grandma gave him threepence a week pocket-money, but it was impossible to relate that to buying anything beyond marbles he would never play with, a toy soldier with a khaki neck and a pink collar. He brooded upon it emotionlessly, it was like the broad sky over this flat landscape with low houses and wide streets, it was there, a fact, not a problem.

Apart from her hoard, and a small mending basket, and an astounding array of bright aluminium pans that Grandma was *not* going to give up as scrap metal to Save Britain, Grandma's house was bare; there were no spare bits of material, there was no Glory Hole where a boy might root in hope, dawdle over discoveries, no rusting airgun to stop the heart, no old walking boots to arouse heroic dreams of striding over the sandhills, surefooted, and no gritty socks to shake out after. Her house was clean, scrubbed, polished, tidied up.

'You've brought that blasted gasmask case in again.' His understanding of the monologue was glancing; certainly there was mention of a gasmask case, and it came out of the teacher's face, not seen well, not reaching any responding chord in the boy; merely a face, making sounds. 'Twenty-five lines by tomorrow morning.'

The boy had a vague notion of what this meant, some recollection that it was to do with writing. You were made to stand out in front of the class, and the others would try to catch your eye and make you giggle – not

in this school though, that was primary school at home
– or you were sent to march along the corridor past
shouting classrooms to the headmaster's office, and a
silence emphasized by fat brutish fingers scratching
with a steel pen at remarkably clean paper. In the class-
room there was very little paper, here there were shelves
full of thick wads of it, all clean. Looking back, the
headmaster must have been a hoarder, like Grandma.
After a long wait, your socks easing down your calves,
the headmaster would enquire, and you replied in murmured monosyllables; then he hit you hard on the palms
of your hands with a ruler, three on each palm. Or you
got lines, lines to write, in ink they had to be, on a piece
of paper. 'I must not . . .' I must not what?

After the sing-song, the matter of the lines came back
to him, briefly. It was not within Grandma's experience
to be at school still at eleven; she couldn't think what
more there was to do in a school further than her own
excellent penmanship and a shrewd perception of add-
ing up and subtraction. Long division and multiplica-
tion were not even words in her vocabulary. To explain
to her that his gasmask case smelt unpleasant to the
teacher, and that this had somehow resulted in his having to write something twenty-five times, in ink, was like
taking a run-up to jump the Grand Canyon. He'd seen
a small picture of the Grand Canyon, along with Niagara
Falls and some other miniaturized wonders, on a page
in one of his encyclopaedias; there was a very very small
man on a pony in the picture, to show how vast the
Canyon was. Nor was there paper in the house that he
could see. The only pen he knew of was in his desk, at
school. Taking a pen home was expressly forbidden.
The twenty-five lines joined the gasmask case in the
grey back of his mind, inert, insoluble.

'*Fifty* lines,' said the teacher on the Monday. He made

no mention of the smell, perhaps he'd got used to it. Other children surrounded him at playtime and called him stinker, but lost interest when he seemed indifferent to their screeching: he *was* indifferent, except that their taunt joined a galaxy of other unexplained events which added up to nothing. How had the teacher remembered the lines? Another mystery. Out of more than forty children jammed together, the teacher could remember one; where the boy, who sat among them, stood watching them hurl themselves demented about the playground, sang with them all afternoon, had not the smallest acquaintance with any of them; he heard their names recited every morning, and knew not one. Sometimes a name would take his interest: 'Hamnet?' 'Here sir', but the voice was behind him, the face hidden, the identity unrevealed ...

'A hundred lines.'

The teacher conveyed no impression of annoyance, was preoccupied, his eyes took in the boy and then passed on, brisk.

'Five hundred lines.'

There had been a weekend in between, walking for days, it seemed, on the beach, nourished by a triangular stick of purple fruit-flavoured ice bought on the promenade from a youth with a bicycle which had an ice-box fixed in front of the handle-bars, and little black iron legs to keep the machine upright as he served. 'Stop Me And Buy One' it said on the box, so he did. The lad gave him a piece of strange ice which he held in the palm of his hand until it disappeared in a final squiggle, like tiny sky-writing. Then he chewed on the block, keeping it clear of his fillings.

The beach was cold and horizonless, empty, but the bits of deckwood gave him stories of submarines and seamines, and there were tree-stumps, carved and polished by the distant tide, bleached bones and starfish. Every Saturday and every Sunday his Grandma asked him did he want an apple and a sandwich or a bit of pie to take if he was going to be out all day; every Saturday and every Sunday she scolded him mildly for not coming back for a bite. Or so it seemed, the days were one with the beach, endless and cold.

The sister must have found some friends in the street, he saw little of her. Grandma was impatient with her faddiness, as she named it, and failed to detect the unhappiness it represented; she would screw the child's lustrous brown hair into tight, mean pigtails: 'Tidier that way', perhaps screwing up her own golden youth and taming it. Offhand, and without hope of success, the boy opened drawers and cupboards in one of Grandma's brief absences from the house: no writing paper, no pen, no ink; an indelible pencil behind the clock, sheaves of white tissue paper enfolding scarves, slips, 'Too good to wear'.

'A thousand lines, son.'

How many was a thousand? Walking back from primary school, he once counted backwards from a hundred, walking along a rough unmade road beneath trees which met overhead, and he lost count because a blackbird shouted at him; certainly the backward-counting had taken a long time. His contemplation of the thousand lines, whose content he did not know, and which he was never going to write, ran parallel and under a further remark of the teacher's, also addressed to him:

' . . . and you stay here after the sing-song till you've done them.'

Happiness, real, indestructible happiness welled up in the boy's skull, clearing his eyes: he looked at the teacher and saw him distinctly for the first time, understood his surroundings. He had been set a task he knew he could do, and with refreshed mental appetite thirsted for further information. 'What shall I write, sir?'

Looking back forty years later, I realize with a start that the teacher had entirely forgotten the misdemeanour. The boy never knew. The teacher stared at the boy, crammed children murmured of other matters, but it must have seemed to the teacher that the tiller had slipped from his hand, and that the susurrus was mutinous: he spoke without confidence, his eyes vague, his brow furrowed in racing concentration. 'I must not misbehave. In class.' The words sounded silly in the teacher's mouth, he looked sharply about for mockery, every private smirk seemed to test the thin ice of his authority. 'Something amusing you, Schofield?'

'No sir.'

'Perhaps you'd like to tell us all.'

'No sir, I mean nothing, sir, I mean ...'

'*What* d'you mean?'

'Don't know, sir.'

The class was silent, the teacher satisfied.

At playtime, the boy saw his sister by the railings.

'Hello,' he said.

'Hello.'

'I've got to stay in after school.'

'Oh,' she said.

The boy was me.

A LIFE

The dog started a rabbit. It ran straight, and low to the ground. I fired, went to pocket it, dismantled the gun, stowing it in the pouches under my coat, stock, barrels, forepiece, a business of seconds when I'm on land where I don't have permission. In any case, nobody really hears one shot, it's the second shot that has the farmer out in the yard for a look. I don't much notice how cold or warm I am until I've got something for the pot, but I found myself sweaty from the climb, and chilled now.

On the lower, green slopes a tiny figure, with two plastic carrier bags, tramping diagonally upwards. I could see no detail, but a mile away she was clear in my mind. Frances. Bare-legged, a light fawn overcoat, her thick hair duller now, once straw-yellow, wild about her shoulders. The mist of rain swept down and I lost her from sight. As a schoolchild she ran barefoot down the meadow carrying shoes and socks, always a bright clean frock; at the stream, she sat and washed her feet, rubbed herself dry on the socks, donned them, and the shoes, and ran on for the bus. Every schoolday.

The rain was coming at me horizontal and icy out of Yorkshire, gripping me between collar and hat with steel fingers that made my skull ache. The whaleback of Pike Hill disappeared from the moorland horizon in a sheet of driving grey as I came down to the rough sunken lane that goes by Monk Farm; mostly derelict now, but enough shelter in the little barn for me to hesitate, and then go in. The dog stood in the yard for a minute or so, then came into the barn by me and curled up tight at my feet, nose under its tail. The word is Monk Farm was first built as a religious foundation. Tucked into a hollow, it still takes the North East wind full on the gables. Must have been a Mad Monk. Now Frances lets the grazing out to others, for a small cash rent. Her father, now long dead, told me they slept with thick mufflers round their heads against the shrieking roar of the wind in winter. One thorn tree, black and crabbed, in spring a huge posy of white blossom, smelling lightly of almonds. Frances lives, as far as you can tell from the outside, in one room, maybe nine feet by nine; the room above has one small broken window, but the stone-flagged roof is still sound, the ridge as straight as when it was built, two hundred years ago.

There was a glimmer of light, and the windows, set in deep mullions, were misted. She must have reached home as I came down. Every day, she carries small packets of wood back from building sites, dead branches picked in the sparse woods along the valley bottom, offcuts from the pallet works. The rabbit's head stuck out of my pocket; I don't like everybody in the village to know all my business, and was puzzled at its size; I drew it out, still warm. It was a hare. A fool that goes hunting and doesn't know the difference between the running of a hare and that of a rabbit. I put it in an inside pocket. The walls of the barn are over three feet thick; the pointing, if ever there was any, scoured away from between the huge weather-darkened pink and yellow sandstone blocks. Where it's broken you can see the rubble filling. Water dripped from my hat, I took it off. Found a dry tissue and wiped over the gun barrels.

Her brother is a stocky man, quite bald, with a fair bristle moustache; Tub, they call him. He lives with the elder sister. Late nights I hear him cursing her in a blur of drunken rage. With men, he's more civil, and told me, with an air of Christian forbearance, how Frances comes to her Sunday tea with them. The elder sister won't answer the door if Tub isn't back from the Shanter, and Frances has to sit on the doorstep until he comes home. I think I'd be made uneasy too by her intense silence, her unkempt look. The sister lays down a loaded plate, Frances comes forward from the chair by the door, takes up the food, and knife and fork, and walks into the scullery. When they've finished, her plate is by the sink, polished clean. She sits a while, and then goes.

The barn must be the oldest part of the farm. The party walls are interwoven hazel sticks, daubed with wattle and then roughly plastered over with lime. I've never seen hazel growing in the valley. Also, one of its windows has been given a carved surround, short barley sugar columns, and a small arch at the top. The local stone, millstone grit, is soft, only just capable of taking an inscription for a headstone, certainly nothing for carving: the layers flake off.

She's a well-made woman, slim and small-breasted, has neat, square hands, a firm chin. She's had lovers over the years. Matt Jones, wholesale butcher. Parked his van, and walked the long field path to her door, straddle legged: not a hillside man. Wednesdays. Half-day closing in Manchester. It was never much spoken of, and, mysteriously, she never had a child.

A clear lozenge beginning to show in the condensation on each window. Any smoke from the stack would be carried away by the weather, but she must have stoked the fire up. With her wood. She buys no newspaper, has no radio, no TV, the house is silent. In what form does she build her thoughts? A hare will keep its habits, even from generation to generation ... This is the only explanation I can find for seeing a jack hare on the same run year after year. And a hare with a dog on it finds its way with grace and ease over the land it knows, even though its eyes are turned in its head to see the dog behind it. I know this last bit is so, because one hare ran straight at me without veering: it wasn't looking forward. Is Frances' mind a wordless space, aware only of clouds or sunshine, vertical bars of mist passing below the farm, speaking of a bright day to follow, fine-ribbed ice on the puddles, new grass between the stones, the slow munch of cows, the ruffle of a jay settling on the roof, one more to come, the reek where a fox has gone by? I know how empty of small everyday concerns my mind can be on the hillside. I get home with slutch up to the knees, and wonder how it got there, where a couple of dots of dirty water on my toecaps will catch my eyes in a busy street.

I moved out into the yard. The dog stirred and shook itself, stretched its stiff limbs back and forward like a ballet dancer, sniffed about. The rain had lifted, the wind bated. The centre window was almost entirely cleared. She sat bolt upright, still in her coat, at a small table covered with old, cracked lino. A tall brass paraffin lamp, smoking a little and darkening the glass chimney more. I stepped closer. She was motionless, hands laid before her on the table top, palms down. No detectable movement of the ribcage, no pulse at the throat that I could see. I felt my lips tighten across my teeth as if they were somebody else's. The heavy iron bars of the fire glowed scarlet, the fire fierce up the chimney. The walls of the little room so stacked with wood they were invisible, except for a space for the door to be opened: you couldn't even tell where the wood had come from to make the fire. Otherwise there was nothing, no cupboard, no chair other than the one she sat on, no rug on the stone floor, greasy and dark with ancient filth, no sign of the carrier bags, no *bed*.

Suddenly she got up and went towards the door at the back. I became aware that my heart was hammering, and pent breath whistled out of me. The room was so completely simple that I stared into it, unable to move.

'What is it you want?'

The words encompassed my head, bouncing back off the walls of farmhouse and barn. Clear, strong, more like a statement than a question. She must have come out through the side door, she was standing in the cobbled yard, ten feet from me. The longer I left it, the bigger the clangour of her question, the more impossible to answer. She looked me in the eyes full; perhaps because she spoke so rarely, words were important, eyes and words burned. I sketched a smile, and felt myself to be a hypocrite, turned away head down, took the lane to the village.

'What is it you want?'

There comes a point in self-neglect, you may not have experienced it, and you may think this is irrelevant: I'm not talking here just about Frances, I'm also talking about myself: there comes a point in self-neglect when to behave as other people do is harder than to go on as you are. Clean underwear, underwear at all, is not a fact. A cracked teacup, with dead tea in it, brown ring, oily surface, can stay where it is. You can shit in a field and use dockleaves. In the end the people you knew as a child have no common subject of conversation with you; even the weather has a different meaning for you; passers-by in the lanes will be uncertain how to greet you; and still the tiny yellow and purple flowers come and go among the hard grass.

I had to be away from home for nearly two months. Returning, I sat with Tub on the bus. He had a new suit,

I could smell the warehouse smell, new leather briefcase on his knee, well-brushed trilby.

'Just been to see my stockbroker.'

An unanswerable remark. 'Oh,' I said.

'You'll know that Frances has gone dead?'

'I'm sorry to hear that. She did no harm.'

'I had the clearing of the house to do. You wouldn't believe the mess. She didn't so much as own a broom. And soap was a dirty word to Frances. You won't be seeing so much of me in the Shanter these days. I tend to use the Conservative Club more.'

I knew he'd tell me in the end, but he was beginning to grind on my nerve ends.

'Monk Farm fetched fifty-eight grand. Architect it is that's got it. Reckons it's a jewel. You should see his car.'